1350

F
BYA

Byars, Betsy

The Glory girl

$12.95

DATE			

The Glory Girl

The GLORY Girl

BETSY BYARS

The Viking Press, New York

First published in 1983 by The Viking Press
40 West 23rd Street, New York, New York 10010
Published simultaneously in Canada by Penguin Books Canada Limited
Printed in U.S.A.
10 9 8 7 6 5 4

Library of Congress Cataloging in Publication Data
Byars, Betsy Cromer.   The glory girl.
Summary: Anna Glory, the one nonsinging member of a gospel-singing
family, feels left out, like her misfit Uncle Newt, until the day
the family bus is involved in a terrible accident.
[1. Family life—Fiction.   2. Singers—Fiction.
3. Traffic accidents—Fiction]   I. Title.
PZ7.B9836Gl   1983   [Fic]   83-5927   ISBN 0-670-34261-0

TO ALAN MYERS

Contents

Contents

The
Blue
Bus

The Glory family bus rumbled along the highway. The old tires wobbled. The engine missed. The windows and doors rattled. From time to time there was a loud bang as the engine backfired.

Anna Glory was stretched out on one of the back seats of the bus, trying to sleep. She lay on her side with her coat over her like a blanket. Down the aisle the pale blue outfits of the Glory Gospel Singers waved and swayed on coat hangers, giving off the faint odor of sweat and Right Guard.

The music her family had sung that night still sounded

in Anna's head. The songs had been written that way—to start hands clapping, feet tapping, to make people want to join in on the chorus.

> *When He calls me,*
> *Calls me,*
> *Calls me,*
> *I will answer,*
> *Answer,*
> *Answer,*
> *And I'll never,*
> *Never,*
> *Never,*
> *Answer, "No."*
> *Yes, when He calls me*
> *Calls me,*
> *Calls me . . .*

Anna closed her eyes. The music, the lights, the clapping, swaying crowd—it all seemed the way life was meant to be. And she at the back of the auditorium, waiting to sell Glory albums and cassette tapes at intermission—she felt left out, not just from the music and the crowd, but somehow from the rest of the world.

Anna sighed. She shifted on the hard seat. The Glory bus had once been a school bus, and the seats were worn slick from years of sliding, restless children.

Anna was the only person in the history of the Glory family who could not carry a tune. There had been a brief time, when Anna was seven, when it had been hoped that she could learn to play the drums.

Waiting for the drums to be delivered had been the happiest time of Anna's life. She had imagined how important she would look, beating time on the silver-and-blue Wilson drums, crossing her arms different ways, hitting this drum and that one.

But when the drums came and Anna held the sticks at last, she discovered that she could no more beat time than she could sing. She was clumsy. The drumsticks clattered to the floor. Again and again her father shouted, "Anna, listen to the music!"

And finally the drums had gone to the twins. They, at age five, took to it like monkeys, and before the week was out, they were playing as if they had been doing it all their lives.

"Anyway, darling," her father had said, "we need you to sit in the back and sell records."

"I don't want to sell records," she'd said, starting to cry.

He'd looked at her. None of the children ever whined or pleaded when their father got that expression on his face. "You'll get used to it," he had said, and then turned away.

It had been five years, however, and Anna had not gotten used to it yet.

She glanced up the aisle, past her mother's head, which was lolling over the edge of the seat, past the twins' legs kicking at each other, past the gold of Angel's hair, to her father. Mr. Glory was driving the bus, holding a Pall Mall cigarette between his teeth. He had to steer with his whole body.

Lately the blue bus had started to take on a will of its own. It went left when it was supposed to go right, swerved into the dirt beside the road for no reason, and Mr. Glory had to be ready for these unexpected moves. Mr. Glory sometimes seemed to be dealing with a team of willful mules instead of a bus.

He trusted the bus, though. "It gets us there," he would say when it was criticized for dying down at intersections or for stopping short and causing Mrs. Glory to slide out of her seat. Mr. Glory was proud that the bus had never had a flat, an oil change, or a breakdown in all the years he had been driving it.

Anna's eyes closed. Pall Mall smoke drifted to the back of the bus and hung in the stale, cold air. On wet days Anna felt she could smell old peanut butter sandwiches and sneakers, and if she reached down under the seats she could feel knots of bubble gum so old they were as hard as the metal.

The Glory family's songs seemed to hang in the still cold air of the bus, too.

> *Sing with the Glorys*
> *Yes, come sing*

With the Glorys
If you sing
With the Glorys
Then you'll never
Sing a-lone.

When Anna heard that song, the Glory Gospel Singers' theme song, the last number on the program, she would get up and move to the aisle where everybody could see her. Her father would step closer to the microphone, his guitar shifted out of the way, on his hip.

"Yes, ladies and gentlemen, if you've enjoyed listening to the songs of the Glory Gospel Singers tonight—well, you can have all the songs you've heard on one long-playing album or cassette tape for the low, low price of eight dollars. That's a lot of singing for eight dollars.

"At the back of the auditorium one of the Glory girls, our little Anna—she can't sing, but ain't she pretty?—she'll be waiting to help you with your purchases. Hold up your hand, darling, so they can see where you're at."

Dutifully Anna would hold up her hand, wave, and then move back out of the light.

"And in the meantime, folks, remember, all the Glory family—Maudine, the twins Joshua and Matthew, our lead singer Angel, and yours truly, John Glory—want you to—"

While Mr. Glory was introducing the family, Anna

would sit at her table and unlock her cash box. She would straighten the stacks of records and cassette tapes as inside the auditorium the music swelled.

Sing with the Glorys
Yes, come sing
With the Glorys
If you sing
With the Glorys
Then you'll never,
Never,
Never!
Siiiinnnnnng a-lone!

On the back seat of the bus Anna pulled her coat up around her neck. She closed her eyes. Her body slid on the worn seat as the old bus stubbornly swerved to the left for no reason, and Mr. Glory, with a puff on his Pall Mall, brought it back to the road again.

A
Secret
Letter

The neighbors complained about the Glorys' house. There was no grass in the front yard. A second school bus, also painted blue, was on concrete blocks in the side yard. Kudzu vines crept closer every summer and had already captured the pine trees in the back.

When the Glorys were away, the house looked as if it had been abandoned. When they were at home, the noise, the shouting, the singing, and the quarreling made it seem that the house had been invaded by rowdies.

Mr. Glory steered the bus into the dirt driveway, past some ragged azaleas, which were wrapped with old scraps of paper and leaves, and came to a shuddering stop by the worn chinaberry tree.

"We're home," he said tiredly. It was five o'clock in the morning.

The Glory family began to struggle up from their sleeping positions. "Boys," Mrs. Glory said. She automatically puffed her beehive hairdo as she sat up. She was only four feet eight inches tall, and she was proud of her hairdo, which made her five feet three. "Boys!"

"I'm up, " Joshua lied sleepily. He thought he was in his bed and she was calling him to get ready for school.

"We're home!" She shook them with one hand—her other was still on her hair. The twins popped up like birds in a nest. Their hair, pasted down earlier with Brylcreem, stood up like wire.

"Angel," Mrs. Glory said more gently.

Angel was the beauty of the family. She was on the third seat, still sleeping like a baby. Her hand rested on her cheek, her thumb touched her lips. Her real name was Brenda, but nobody, not even her teachers, called her anything but Angel.

One by one, the Glorys staggered down the bus steps and walked to the house. The frosted weeds crunched beneath their feet. Their breath froze in the early morning air.

Mrs. Glory was carrying the costumes, holding them over her arm more carefully than she had carried any of her babies. When one of the twins bumped sleepily against her in the dark, she said sharply, "Don't touch!" and swatted at him, hitting only the cold air.

"Missed me," Matthew said, yawning, half asleep.

Anna walked beside her father. He was puffing on another Pall Mall. Mr. Glory seemed to go to seed after a performance. He would leave the stage, his handsome face shining with the joy of religion, and then three hours later his gray whiskers would have popped out and his eyes would be baggy and his curly hair as greasy and limp as it had been when he was sixteen.

Behind them, the motor of the Glory bus gave one last rattle, shaking like a sick mule. Anna glanced back. She couldn't remember that happening before.

"Just settling down," her father explained mildly. He opened the door of the house, tossed his cigarette into the weeds, and entered. "Nobody has to go to school today," he announced as he picked up the mail.

"Will you give me a note?" Joshua asked. "I got Miss McElhaney this year, and if we don't have a note we get a zero."

Mr. Glory did not glance up. In the doorway Mrs. Glory nodded that she would give him a note. Then she peered at the thermostat, turned it up, and the heat came on in the basement with a small explosion.

Anna moved to stand over the register. As the hot air bellowed her skirt, she felt comfortable for the first time that evening. "That feels good."

Mr. Glory did not look up. He was sorting the mail,

peering hard at each envelope. He slid the bills into a drawer, pushing the unpaid ones already there to the back to make room. The letters he put in a neat stack in front of him.

He lit a cigarette. He inhaled. He opened the first letter.

"Lions Club wants us for a benefit in Walhalla," he said as he exhaled. Anna nodded. He opened the second letter. His voice rose slightly. "PTA's asking about a possible fund raiser in Due West."

"That's good."

"And . . ." He paused as he opened a third letter. "And we're invited to the Gospel Jubilee in Asheville in June."

He opened the last letter. He was holding his cigarette between his teeth now, allowing himself to smile. The only time Mr. Glory looked happy at home was when he read the mail and scheduled their appearances.

His eyes slid down the page of the fourth letter, checking for important information—the date, place, money. Suddenly he frowned. He began puffing on his Pall Mall so hard that for a moment his features disappeared in smoke.

"Who is that one from?" Anna asked. She knew from the intensity of his frown that it was not good news. Her father did not answer. He was staring at the letter as if it were in a foreign language.

"Dad, is something wrong?"

Mr. Glory looked up then. His eyes were chips of steel. "Why aren't you in bed?"

"I wanted to get warm first." She did not move. She felt her father owed her an answer about the letter. She had sold twenty-eight albums and thirty-four cassette tapes that night—a new record. And all he had said was, "From now on, you ought to sell that many every night."

She cleared her throat. "So who is the letter from?"

"I said go to bed, Anna."

Having an argument with Mr. Glory was like going down the basement stairs, with the air getting colder on each step. She tried one last time. "Dad—"

He looked at her, and without a word Anna turned and walked to the bedroom she shared with Angel. She sat down heavily on the bed. "He makes me so mad."

"Who?"

"Him!"

Angel turned back to her mirror. She was rolling her hair, the thick, golden, Rapunzel-like tresses, on fat plastic rollers. Carefully she pinned a roller into place. No matter what time the Glory family got home, no matter how tired she was, Angel always rolled her hair.

"I just wanted to know what one letter said, one stupid letter, and he gave me his deep-freeze look and said, 'Go to bed, Anna.' " She sighed. "And, listen, Angel, I spent the whole night freezing in the back of that auditorium. There was no heat at all, and I didn't complain once."

She looked at Angel resentfully as she kicked off her

shoes. "You don't know how it feels because you're up on the stage. You've got the lights on you. You're never cold." She pulled off her sweater and slipped out of her skirt. "I'm back there in the dark, shivering, the orphan child."

"You're not an orphan."

"Well, that's what it feels like."

Angel wound a stray hair around a roller. She loved her hair. She didn't know how people who didn't have nice hair amused themselves. "Maybe . . ." she said thoughtfully. Then abruptly her eyes went back to her hair. Her doll-like face smiled back at her in the mirror.

"Maybe what?" Anna asked. She pulled her nightgown over her head and got under the covers in one motion. "Brrrrr." She looked at her sister. "Maybe what?" she asked again. "Angel!" Sometimes Angel clicked off in the middle of a conversation, just sort of disappeared, leaving Anna with the feeling she was talking to a blank wall. "Maybe what, Angel?"

"Oh, nothing. Just about the letter. Maybe something's wrong. That's all."

Watching her sister, Anna felt a chill that was more than the sheets. Angel, with her dreamy eyes, could sometimes see into the future with amazing clarity.

"Like what? What could be wrong?"

"I don't know."

"Have you heard anything? Do you—"

12

"Oh, let me alone. You know I can't talk when I'm rolling my hair."

Anna drew the covers up around her neck. She watched as Angel, smiling slightly, selected another roller. By the time Angel was finished, Anna had fallen asleep.

Downhill
Disaster

Matthew and Joshua, the Glory twins, had as many stitches in them as rag dolls. They were proud of their stitches, too, and kept a record of them. So far, Joshua had forty-nine and Matthew forty-two. Matthew would have had eight or nine more except that Mr. Glory had refused to take him to the hospital the afternoon he skated into the parked pickup truck on Oak Street.

"Stitches cost money," Mr. Glory had said, inspecting the wound coldly. "You boys have to learn that."

"He went into the truck on purpose," Joshua said, looking with envy at Matthew's leg.

"I had to," Matthew whined. "It was the only way I

14

could keep from going onto the highway. What'd you want me to do—get myself killed?''

"I'll close this myself," Mr. Glory said. "Get me the adhesive tape, Joshua.''

"Yes, sir!''

"I want stitches.''

"Do you have any idea how many albums we would have to sell to pay for sewing up that leg? And when I get through, if you bend that knee and open it up . . .''

"What'll you do to him?'' Joshua asked.

Mr. Glory did not answer. He always left his threats hanging. But he applied the tape with such firmness that Matthew had to walk stiff-legged for a week.

This morning, since Matthew didn't have to go to school, he decided to play with a bicycle he had found in the junkyard. The bicycle was old and rusty and had no chain, but Matthew was not discouraged. "Anybody who wants to see me ride better come outside!'' he called to the quiet house.

"I'll watch out the window,'' Anna called from the kitchen. Anna had stayed home today too. Usually she went to school whether she had to or not. School was better in a lot of ways than home. At school she even sang in the chorus, and no one noticed she couldn't carry a tune.

But today Anna wanted to find the letter that had upset her father last night. She was determined to read it.

"Be careful, boys,'' Mrs. Glory called from the bedroom.

Joshua followed his brother slowly into the yard. He did not want to watch, because he was jealous of the bike. Both twins had wanted wheels from the day they were born.

"It won't go," Joshua said. "It hasn't got a chain. That's what makes a bike go, like a motor makes a car go."

Joshua hoped with all his heart this was true. The only reason he was following Matthew was so that, when the bicycle didn't work, he could yell, "I told you so! I knew it wouldn't work!"

Ahead of him, Matthew was pushing the bicycle up the hill. Joshua paused to throw a weed into the air and hit it with an imaginary bat.

"It'll go." Matthew was unconcerned. "The tires are good."

"Tires don't make it go. Chains do. I saw that on TV."

"Liar!" Mr. Glory had removed the channel control on the TV, and the TV was permanently tuned to the religious network. "Anyway, you just wait and see."

"That's what I'm going to do—wait and see you fall on your face."

"And I'm not letting you have a turn."

"I wouldn't ride that heap of junk if you paid me."

They were halfway up the hill now, and Joshua stopped. He watched Matthew and his bicycle for a moment. The bicycle was going sideways. It was like those old grocery carts that keep turning into the stacks of canned goods. It wouldn't go. It couldn't. But just in case . . .

Joshua smiled. He waited until Matthew was intent on his bicycle, and then he slipped behind some bushes. He crouched. He leaned up to peer through the leaves. He had not been seen. He got set to pounce.

At the top of the hill Matthew was turning his bicycle around. He eased one leg over the seat as carefully as if he were getting on a strange horse. "I'm ready," he called down the now empty hill.

No answer.

"Where are you, Josh? Don't you want to see me ride my bicycle?"

No answer.

"All right, then, you're going to miss it. Anna, watch! I'm starting. Joshua, you better look if you want to see me."

He pushed off. His start was ragged. His front tire dug into the earth like a plow. He was glad Joshua hadn't seen that. He lifted the bike out of its rut and pushed. The front tire began to roll. "Here I come!"

His voice rose as the bicycle picked up speed. "I'm really coming! Look, Josh, look!"

The front wheel struck a rock and wobbled, causing the bike to weave from side to side. "Whoa!" Matthew cried. His feet found the pedals and, forgetting there was no chain, he began to pedal. "Yikes!" He held his legs out at the sides. He pushed first with one foot and then the other. The bicycle picked up more speed.

"Josh, it works!" he yelled happily.

Behind the bush Joshua was ready. His eyes shone with pleasure. He shifted nervously. He was intent on one thing—his brother weaving down the hill on that bicycle.

He duck-walked forward two steps. Matthew's happy yells came closer. "Look, Joshua!" He was yelling, pleading now. "Look at me!"

"I'll look all right," Joshua said, smiling to himself.

The bicycle was almost at the bush now. With a gasp of anticipation, Joshua jumped out, screaming. He was directly in front of the bicycle, in a crouch, his arms outstretched. He was as ready as a lineman for the Pittsburgh Steelers.

"Yannnnnnnnnngh!" he cried.

He had a moment of intense pleasure as he saw Matthew's startled expression. The bicycle hit a rock—Joshua hadn't known that would happen—things were getting better and better. His eyes gleamed as the bicycle swerved to the right and wobbled back and forth on the rocky ground.

"Hah!" he cried triumphantly.

He was planning to add a second, "Hah!" but suddenly the bicycle was no longer wobbling. It was coming straight for him. Over the handlebars he saw Matthew's face white with alarm.

"Hey, watch out! Look where you're—"

Joshua broke off. He struggled to get up and failed. He scrambled backward. He stumbled. He threw up his hands to protect his face and then, in a crouch, took the impact

18

of the front wheel directly in the chest.

He screamed. He fell backward, kicking out like a Russian dancer. Then he was thrown onto his back. He twisted sideways to save himself, but the bicycle came after him. It was like an enraged bull.

"Aiiiiii," he screamed as the bicycle caught up with him and rode over his head. Chainless, it poked fourteen holes into his scalp.

"*Aiiiiiiiiiiiiiiiiiiiiii* . . ."

The bicycle swerved to the right then and crashed into the dead kudzu vines. Joshua's scream went on and on in the still, cold air.

Matthew came up out of the dead vines, slow and mad. He had no idea of the damage the bicycle had done. He thought it was another one of Joshua's tricks. Joshua was always pretending to be hurt worse than he was.

"What'd you do that for?" he yelled at his brother. "You made me wreck, you stinking—"

He did not finish his insult because at that moment he saw his brother. Matthew stood, drawing in one long breath, his hands clasped over his mouth.

Joshua was twisting like a beached fish, throwing himself so violently from side to side that he was sliding down the hill. His hands clutched his head. Blood was streaming from each of the fourteen holes, running through his fingers, down his trembling hands.

Matthew began screaming then, too, but his was a quiet in-and-out sound. He was used to the sight of blood—they both were—but not this much, and not from the head. Matthew could not move. He had not known a head could hold so much blood. He had thought there was nothing up there but brains.

Finally he got his voice. "Mommmmmmmm!" He turned and began to run down the hill. His knees were so wobbly that he jerked along like a puppet.

He saw Anna coming out the back door, and he changed his cry to "Annaaaaaaaa!" She ran toward him. Behind her was Mr. Glory.

"What is it? What have you boys done now? I told you I wanted some peace this morning. I told you I needed to think. You—"

As Anna passed Matthew, he pointed up the hill to where his brother lay. "Joshua," he gasped. "Joshua's scalped!"

Anna's
Search

Anna stood at the window with one arm around Matthew's shoulders. They had been standing there ever since Mr. and Mrs. Glory had left for the hospital with Joshua.

"It's my fault if he dies," Matthew said glumly.

"Joshua's not going to die."

"How do you know that? You're not a doctor."

"I saw him. I was the first one there, remember? I helped Mom wash his head."

Matthew was silent for a moment. Then he said, "His eyes . . . that's what makes me think he's going to die."

The memory of his brother being carried to the bus came

21

back to him. Joshua's head had been wrapped in a pink bloodstained towel, his face had been a small, pale circle, his arms dangled at his sides.

His eyes had been rolled back into his head. That was what really scared Matthew. It was as if Joshua were trying to see how much damage had been done inside his head.

Those sightless eyes had made Matthew feel bad enough to be taken to the hospital too, a second patient. "This one was run over by a bicycle," his parents would tell the doctors. "This one is just plain sick."

Anna turned away from the window with a sigh. She felt she needed to do something to take her mind off Matthew. Her glance fell on her father's desk. It was then that she remembered the letter.

"Where are you going, Anna?" Already Matthew missed the comfort of her arm.

"Just over here."

She walked to the desk and pulled open a drawer. She looked through the contents and slammed it shut. She opened a second drawer.

The noise caused Matthew to turn around. He watched with growing alarm as he saw Anna going through their father's desk. This was something so forbidden that even he and Joshua had never done it.

"What are you doing?"

"Looking for something." Anna did not glance up. She shuffled through some papers.

"What?"

"A letter."

"Dad will be mad at you for going through his things."

"Who's going to tell him?"

She looked at Matthew then, hard, over an open drawer, and he turned away with a sigh. "Not me," he said tiredly. Suddenly he felt as if it should be bedtime. He actually wanted to go to bed for the first time in his life. "What time is it?"

"Eleven o'clock."

"At night?"

"Matthew, look outside! It's broad daylight!"

"Well, I'm tired. I feel like—"

He glanced down and saw that his pants were covered with drops of his brother's blood. When had that happened? He pulled up his pants legs. His sneakers too. He could not remember when he had been close enough to Joshua for— Oh, yes, when his parents were carrying Joshua down the hill. He had helped them, or tried to, until his father told him to get out of the damn way. It was the first time Matthew had ever heard his father curse, and he had gotten out of the way immediately. He had run ahead and opened the kitchen door.

"Do you think Josh's going to die?" he asked Anna. His interest in the desk search was gone. He stared at the empty road.

"No."

"I do."

"Matthew, scalp wounds always bleed like that. A boy

23

in my room hit his head on the pencil sharpener, a little wound, no deeper than that, and he bled all over the whole school. And Joshua had about a dozen wounds like that. Anyway, I had a good look at him when we were washing his head, and they were just punctures.''

She slammed the drawer of unpaid bills shut, saw that two letters had fallen to the floor and picked them up. "It's got to be here," she said, discarding them.

"What?"

"The letter!"

"Oh."

Matthew felt as tired and confused as an old person. He felt like Grandpa Glory, who couldn't keep anything straight. Grandpa Glory had never even understood that he and Joshua were twins—he thought they were just one boy who was real active. "Here you are again," he was always saying.

"Listen, Matthew, maybe you can help me. Last night Dad got a letter, and it made him furious, and he wouldn't tell me who it was from." She straightened. "I have a right to know what's going on in this family. You do too. We have a right to see that letter!"

"Not me."

Matthew had had all the trouble he wanted for one day. He looked back at the road. All he wanted was for Joshua to come home and for it to be bedtime.

"What are you looking for?" Angel said. She came into the room, brushing her hair. She was getting ready to wash it and then roll it again. Sometimes Anna asked her, "Why on earth do you roll your hair at night when you're going to wash it the next morning?" But Angel never explained. Anna had plain brown hair, and Angel felt she would not understand.

"I want to see that letter!" Anna said. She opened the top drawer again and slammed it shut. "Remember, I was telling you last night that Dad got a letter?"

"Oh, that. It's in his jacket."

"His jacket? How do you know?"

"I saw him reading it this morning, and then he goes and stuffs it in his pocket. You're practically sitting on it right now."

"This jacket?" The jacket was slung over the back of the chair. Anna patted the pockets until she heard the rustling of paper. Her eyes gleamed as she pulled out the letter. "Aha!"

She smoothed the letter over her knees. "It's from Uncle Newt!" She began to read to herself. "Guess what?" She read a few more lines. She was moving her lips now. She glanced up. "No wonder Dad was upset."

"You better put the letter back," Angel said. "The bus is coming."

"The bus is a million miles away, in the hospital parking lot. Guess what?"

"What?"

"Uncle Newt's getting out of prison!"

"It *is* the bus!" Matthew cried at the door. "I see it!"

He pressed his face against the glass. "Only I don't see Josh. Maybe Josh died. Maybe—"

Anna stuffed the letter back into her father's pocket and stood up quickly. "I'm glad you two have good hearing. I'm beginning to think I'm deaf. A teacher in second grade did tell me I needed to have my hearing checked."

"They always tell me that too." Angel moved to the door to watch with Matthew.

"There he is!" Matthew screamed. "He's alive!"

Relief flooded through his body so fast it left him weak. He held onto the doorknob.

"He's sitting up!" He made it sound like a miracle. "And he's eating something! Ice cream!"

His joyful screams filled the house. He spun around. "Ice cream!" He flung open the door and filled his lungs with cold November air.

He stood, grinning, as the bus rolled up beside the worn chinaberry tree and came to its usual shuddering stop.

"They're home!"

As Matthew crossed the porch, hopping with excitement, he suddenly paused. He wondered if Joshua would remember the last words he, Matthew, had said. His smile faded slightly. He wrapped one arm around the post. He ran his foot back and forth over the warped floorboards.

This had happened when his parents had been carrying Joshua to the bus. Matthew had run along beside them. He had been crying, and he really loved his brother for the first time in his life.

Choking with love and fear and remorse, he had cried, "You can have the bicycle. It's yours!"

He wondered if Joshua had heard that. Maybe he hadn't. Maybe he wouldn't remember. Head injuries sometimes caused amnesia. He didn't want Joshua to have amnesia, of course, but he did hope Joshua hadn't heard him.

Maybe it was selfish, maybe it was wrong, but he wasn't through with the bicycle yet. He liked that bicycle. And, after all, if Joshua hadn't gotten in the way with his big head, he would have ridden all the way down the hill on it.

Anna passed him, running toward the bus. She took the steps in one leap. Matthew broke into a grin and followed.

The Phone Call

Oh, we're climbing, climbing, climbing
Every day it's one step more.
Higher, higher, higher
Than we've ever been before.
Looking, looking, looking
For that heavenly shore
That will lead us to the
Kingdom of Love.

The Glory family was singing in the living room, learning a new song, while Anna fixed supper in the kitchen.

The worst thing that could happen to a person in this family, Anna decided as she waited for the water to boil, was not being able to carry a tune or beat time.

Anna lifted the lid on the pot. "Boil!" she told the water. She slammed down the lid.

There were lots of people who didn't fit into their families. Anna reminded herself of this all the time—the dumb one in a family of brains, the ugly one in a family of beauties. But no one—Anna was sure of this—felt as left out as she did when her family sang together.

"Joshua, you're not in rhythm," Mr. Glory said. "Pay attention!"

"I can't!" Joshua wailed, letting his drumsticks drop to his sides. "My head hurts!"

Joshua had had forty-two stitches put in his head the day before, three to close each puncture. Now his head was ringed with gauze, and some of the black strings from the stitches stuck out the bottom.

"Let him go lie down," Mrs. Glory pleaded from the piano bench.

"Those stitches cost me sixty-four dollars!"

"I know that, dear."

Mr. Glory had been in one of his "moods," as Mrs. Glory called them, for two days. Anna knew it was because Uncle Newt was getting out of prison. She had been waiting for his mood to lift so she could bring up the subject.

"I think you boys *try* to be bad," Mr. Glory said.

"I don't," Matthew said.

"Let me tell you there's enough evil in this world without you two adding to it. I read the other day that there's kids in New York City sucking coins out of subway slots. They make a living out of that. And a woman in California is feeding her kids cat food while she eats T-bone steaks. And I—"

Joshua, recognizing the start of a long monologue, interrupted with, "*I* don't try either." Tears began to roll down his cheeks.

Joshua was used to not getting sympathy. Usually when he came in, hurt and crying, Mr. Glory would say, "Well, that's what you get for chasing a Coca-Cola truck."

But yesterday—the sight of himself in the hospital mirror—they had had to bring the mirror to prove to him he had not really been scalped. And as he had looked at himself, his forehead painted yellow, a path shaved through his hair, his head ringed with black stitches, he had felt so sorry for himself that he had cried like a baby. Now he felt fresh sobs shaking his body. His drumsticks clattered to the floor.

Mr. Glory relented. "All right," he said, "go to bed. Take a pain pill."

"Thank you," Joshua said tearfully as he crawled out from under the drum set.

"Can I have a pain pill too?" Matthew asked quickly. "My knee still—"

"No! And these accidents have got to stop! You've had

your last stitch, Joshua, you hear me?''

"Yes."

"I don't care if you split yourself wide open. You too, Matthew."

"Me? He's the one that's got the stitches. He's got ninety-one! I've only got forty-two!" He could not keep the sense of injustice out of his quivering voice.

"Matthew!"

"Yes, sir."

"All right now." Mr. Glory ran his hands through his limp hair. He needed another body permanent. "Now, Angel, after we sing the chorus, you—"

The phone rang, interrupting him. "Get that, Anna," he called.

"It'll be for Angel," Anna said, putting the lid back on the pot. "Some stupid boy. 'You don't know me, but I saw you in the blah . . . blah . . . blah.' " She came out of the kitchen wiping her hands on her jeans.

In the living room Mr. Glory nodded to his wife. "Maudine, let's try it again."

Mrs. Glory began the introduction. She had been playing the piano since she was four years old. She never had to look down at the keys.

" 'Oh, we're climbing, climbing, climbing.' "

Anna picked up the phone in the hall. "Hello."

" 'Every day it's one step more.' "

"What?" Anna asked.

" 'Higher, higher, higher.' "

"Wait a minute, let me close the door. Now, who is this?" she asked.

" 'Than we've ever been before.' "

Anna said, "Oh," as if she'd been stuck with a pin. Slowly she lowered the phone and held it against her chest. Then she lifted it and said, "I'll get my dad, Uncle Newt. Hold on."

She opened the door to the living room. A chill of dread caused her to shudder slightly. "Dad?"

" 'Looking, looking, looking for that heavenly shore—' "

"Dad," she said louder.

"Keep going, Maudine," Mr. Glory said as he walked toward the hall. Mrs. Glory began the second verse with a ripple of chords. "Who is it?"

Anna let out her breath in a rush. "It's Uncle Newt. He says he wrote you a letter and he hasn't heard from you and he's getting out of prison and needs to know if—"

Mr. Glory spun around as if he were looking for someone to strike. Mrs. Glory stopped playing the piano. Angel's high note trailed off.

"Did she say Newt's getting out of prison?" Mrs. Glory asked. She stood up so quickly that the piano stool fell over backwards. "John, you've had a letter from Newt?"

Mr. Glory did not answer. Nostrils flaring, he drew in a breath. He showed his teeth like a dog. When anybody saw Mr. Glory in a rage, they never doubted that people had evolved from animals.

"Newt is on the phone?" Mrs. Glory was having a hard time taking in the news. It was the first time she had heard Newt's name mentioned in years. "Your brother Newt is on the phone?"

"Yes!" Mr. Glory screamed. He was so filled with rage that his face burned. He looked to the right, to the left. Anna thought he was looking for a piece of furniture small enough to smash to splinters. She stepped back out of the way.

"I think he's being paroled, Mom," Anna explained. "He wants to come stay with us for a while. He has to have an approved place." She had gotten this from the letter, but her father wouldn't know that.

"Just when we're beginning to have some success," Mr. Glory said through his teeth. "Just when people are beginning to accept us, to believe in us—you know what a woman in Albemarle told me? She said, 'Your whole family is good—it's in your faces and your voices.' She said, 'It does me good to know there's one Christian family left in the world that—' " He broke off.

Anna said, "Dad, he's waiting."

Mr. Glory struck the nearest wall with his fist and looked up at the ceiling. Then, like a balloon losing air, he sank down onto a chair. "And now, just when it's all beginning to happen for us, Newt gets a parole."

"Dad, he's waiting."

Mr. Glory shook his head. "It's the end of everything."

Anna looked at her mother, her sister. No one moved.

Anna went back and picked up the phone. "Uncle Newt, it's me again, Anna. Dad can't come to the phone right now. You want me to have him call you back? . . . I will. Good-bye."

The Bow-Legged Bank Robber

"Tell me everything you remember about Uncle Newt," Anna said.

"I don't remember anything."

"Angel, you do. Look at me. You always go around pretending you don't know what's going on, and you do! You know every single thing that happens in this family."

After the telephone call Mr. Glory had sent everyone out of the living room so he could think. Now Angel and Anna were in their bedroom with the door shut. They could hear their father pacing back and forth on the worn rug, pausing as he reached the wall and turned. He was puffing so hard on a cigarette that they could smell smoke in their bedroom.

"Well, what *can* you remember?"

"Nothing."

"Leave your hair alone for five seconds. Now look at me and tell me what you remember."

"There's really nothing to tell. Uncle Newt wasn't tall and he wasn't short. He wasn't good-looking and he wasn't ugly. His hair wasn't dark and it wasn't light."

She waved her comb from side to side as she spoke, pointing to opposite walls. "He was the kind of man—well, like if he had kids, his kids would never run around wondering, 'Can I be better than Pa?' You know, like we used to wonder if we could turn out better than Mom? Because there's nothing to be better *than!*"

Anna drew in her breath. She felt as if she herself had just been described. She's not tall and she's not short, and she's not pretty and she's not ugly, and no one will ever run around wondering, "Can I be better than Anna?" because everybody can.

"That's a terrible way to describe somebody," she said, stung.

"This is why I never want to tell you anything. You jump on everything I say."

"Well, it's sad to describe people in negatives. He's not this. He's not that."

"What else are you going to do when there's nothing positive?"

36

Anna's shoulders sagged. "I don't know."

Angel watched Anna. "Oh, all right, I just thought of something. When Uncle Newt robbed the bank—Anna, you have to remember that."

"I don't."

"Everyone was so ashamed. Mom wouldn't show her face in the Piggly Wiggly. She went clear to Anderson to buy groceries where nobody knew her."

Anna shook her head. "I can just barely remember it."

"Well, when Uncle Newt robbed the bank—it was First Federal—he took this fellow with him who had real bowed legs—*real* bowed—you could have thrown a basketball through his knees. And the bank got the whole robbery on video tape."

"So?"

"So Uncle Newt and this man, they had on ski masks so nobody would recognize them, but when they walked out of the bank—still on camera—there were these legs!" Angel made a wide gesture in the air with her comb.

"What about it?"

"Anna, nobody in the bank could have described Uncle Newt. There was nothing to describe. If he hadn't taken the bowlegged man along—well, they would never have gotten caught. If he'd taken somebody else—well, they could have turned out to be . . ." She paused. "Name me some famous bank robbers."

"Bonnie and Clyde."

"They could have turned out to be Bonnie and Clyde."

37

"How do you know all this?"

"I listened, and I remember there was a picture in the afternoon newspaper. 'Have You Seen These Men?' And there were Uncle Newt and this other man in their ski masks. And everybody who saw the picture looked at the bowed legs and said right away, 'Why, that's old So-and-so.' I don't remember his real name. Yes, I do. Legs Somebody. And they went over and arrested Legs and he still had his ski mask in his pocket."

"What about Uncle Newt?"

"He ran off to Las Vegas with his half of the money and was arrested out there. He'd checked into Caesar's Palace under his own name."

"Oh." Even with this information Anna felt she was still searching for Uncle Newt. "He sounds like the kind of man—well, I mean he doesn't sound like a person who would deliberately cause trouble. He just sounds sort of— I don't know—dense, stupid."

"Maybe he is stupid—I don't know. But he's always caused trouble. There's a difference. Like I know a lot of stupid people who never cause trouble—I'm a good example. Did you know that when Uncle Newt was little, he burned down the house?"

"Not on purpose!"

"Well, I don't know if you'd call it on purpose or not. He was under the house burning cobwebs with a candle, for the fun of it. He liked to see the cobwebs melt, he said, and he set the kitchen floor on fire and ran away."

"Little kids do crazy stuff," Anna said. "Look at the things Joshua and Matthew have done."

"Well, that was just one thing. I could keep going all night. He was in the Navy—this was when they were drafting people—and he got off his ship in some place like Manila and didn't get back on. He missed the ship. He said he couldn't find it. It was a battleship, Anna—you know how big those are—and he couldn't find it!"

"Maybe . . ." Anna trailed off. She sat on the bed, slumped forward.

"Anyway, I think it was a relief when he was finally sent to prison."

"Now that *is* a terrible thing to say."

"It wasn't me who said it."

"Who? Dad?"

"The day Uncle Newt was sentenced, I remember this perfectly. I was standing right out there in the hall and the phone rang and it was Grandma Glory. It was right before Christmas. Our tree was up. And without even stopping to say hello, Grandma Glory goes, 'He got seven years.' She was crying so hard I had to ask her to say it twice. And Dad called in from the living room, and he goes, 'How long did he get?' I said, 'Seven years,' and he goes, 'Well, it looks like a merry Christmas after all.' "

A
Missing
Uncle

"Am I allowed to ask a question?" Anna asked.

The Glory family was sitting around a table eating Kentucky Fried Chicken out of boxes. In the Kentucky Fried Chicken parking lot, the blue Glory bus was parked close to the highway so everybody driving past could read what was printed on the side. "The Glory Gospel Singers." Free advertising, Mr. Glory called it. He had painted the uneven white letters himself.

Nobody in the family had done much talking since they left home that morning. They were on their way to pick up Uncle Newt at the bus station in Greenville, and Mrs.

Glory had talked to each of the children before they left. She had made each one promise, even Angel, not to do anything to upset their father.

"Am I allowed to ask a question?"

Mrs. Glory shot Anna a look of warning. "What do you want to ask?"

"I was just wondering if Uncle Newt can sing."

Mr. Glory's head snapped up. "Sing? What has that got to do with anything?"

"I just thought if he could sing—well, you've always said you could use another male voice, and if Uncle Newt can sing—well, he could join the Glory family singers."

"Anna, Newt is a criminal," her father said.

"Not if he's out of prison. You're only a criminal until you've paid for your crime. Then you're just like everybody else."

Her father lowered his chicken leg. He wiped grease off his chin with the back of one hand. His cold eyes never left Anna's face. "Don't try me today."

"I'm not trying you. I just don't see why you're still calling him a criminal."

"Is everybody finished?" Mrs. Glory asked quickly. "Newt's bus'll be getting in. We don't want to be late." She began gathering up the scattered napkins and chicken bones. Then she paused and looked at each of the children. "You know, don't you, that your father is being very generous to Newt—giving him a place to stay, giving him a job working on the bus."

No one commented.

"We are all of us trying to do the Christian thing."

Again no one spoke. Matthew was trying to eat the crust off the rest of the pieces of chicken before Joshua got the idea of doing the same thing. He finished a leg, tossed it back in the box, got another. He felt a stab of joy when Joshua accidentally pulled out that very piece.

"What's going on?" Joshua reached back into the red striped box and pulled out a thigh. "You ate all the crust! You—" He turned to Matthew with his fists clenched.

"Boys, I'm talking to you," Mrs. Glory said.

"Well, he ate all the good part. The only part I like is the outside!"

"Have a piece out of my box."

"But what I don't understand about Newt," Anna began, "is—"

Mr. Glory slapped his long hands on the table and rose. "I would like to go five minutes without talking about Newt!"

He turned and walked to the glass counter. He leaned forward, staring at the cartons of cole slaw and bean salad as if his life somehow depended on the little cups.

"Can I help you?" the waitress asked.

"No!"

Mrs. Glory winced at the fury in that exploded "No!" "Now, listen to me and I mean it," she said in a new lower voice. "No more about Newt."

"Well, just tell me if he can sing," Anna said, "and then I'll shut up." She somehow felt that Newt's troubles might be tied in with the fact that, like her, he was a non-singer in a world of song.

"Yes, Anna, he can sing. He used to be in the Gospel Quartet." She leaned forward. "This thing between Newt and—" She nodded toward her husband. "This thing goes way back. When they were little boys, their mother liked Newt best. No matter what John did—and he was the one that made the good grades and did the chores and went to church. He had medals every single year for perfect church attendance. When he went to 4H camp he even got notes from the counselors that he'd attended services so he could keep his record. But no matter what he did to make them proud, Newt was always Grandma Glory's favorite."

"Why would Newt—" Matthew began. Mrs. Glory signaled him to lower his voice. "Why would Newt be the favorite?" he whispered. "Didn't he burn down the house?"

"We don't *ever* mention that, Matthew."

"But didn't he?" Matthew was genuinely puzzled. He had always thought parents favored the children who caused the least trouble.

Mrs. Glory glanced at her husband's back. "I don't know if I can explain it, but it seemed like Grandma Glory always liked—well, people that couldn't get along in the world. She had a three-legged dog one time and she let

43

him do everything but pull up a chair at the table. It's hard for me to understand because—well, because I like all of you exactly the same.''

''You do not. You like Angel best,'' Joshua said.

The Glory twins had paused in their tug-of-war with the last drumstick. They held it between them, one on each end, fingers dug into the meat, waiting to resume the struggle.

They glanced at Angel. She was idly picking tiny pieces of meat from a bone and putting them in her mouth. She always ate with her fingers but so daintily that no one ever corrected her. It even made people around her, eating with forks, look clumsy and bad-mannered.

''That's true,'' Matthew said. ''You do like Angel best.''

Mrs. Glory hesitated. She had never been a good liar. Already her neck was beginning to redden with the strain. ''I like you all the same.'' The flush moved up to her cheeks.

Mr. Glory saved her by turning suddenly and saying, ''It's time to go to the station.''

''Yes, come on, everybody.''

''It's mine!'' Matthew tore the chicken leg out of Joshua's greasy fingers. ''Nyah!'' He ran for the door with the chicken leg sticking out the side of his mouth like a cigar.

''Don't fall,'' Mrs. Glory called, and as Joshua started after him changed it to, ''Don't push!'' She sometimes felt she could put any verb after ''don't'' and it would fit.

The rest of the Glory family got up, went outside, and

44

followed the twins onto the bus. As they settled in their seats, Mr. Glory began to coax the engine into action. With a loud backfire from the muffler, the bus moved out onto the highway.

"Make him give me that chicken," Joshua whined. "He had more than anybody."

"Boys, share," Mrs. Glory said. Her voice was as hopeless as someone talking to a tornado.

"She said *share*."

"Ow! You're not supposed to hit me until my head heals."

"I can hit *you*, but not your head."

"Who said?"

"Dad."

"Dad, did you say that—"

Mrs. Glory reached over and stopped the rest of the question by squeezing Matthew's hand until the tips of his fingers turned purple. "Ow!" Then there was silence.

Anna sat alone on one of the back seats. She had started to feel a kinship with Uncle Newt that surprised her. She couldn't explain it. She didn't feel that way about the members of her own family. Maybe, she told herself, it was like at the movies when with an awkward yearning she would want the bad guy to get away.

"The bus station's over there," Mrs. Glory said, and Anna sat up straighter. She somehow felt as if she alone would be able to recognize Uncle Newt.

"And there's a bus pulling in," Joshua said.

Mrs. Glory turned in her seat to face the children. "Now, don't anybody mention prison. I mean that. We want Newt to feel at home."

"Can we mention it later?" Joshua asked.

"We'll see."

"After supper?"

"We'll see!"

"Because we're doing reports in school on a relative with an interesting occupation, and I'm doing Uncle Newt and bank robbery—and don't you steal my idea, you!"

He gave a warning jab to his brother without making contact.

"This *must* be his bus," Anna said. Her excitement was rising. She moved down the aisle, holding onto the seats so she could be the first one off the bus. She ran across the parking lot and got to the door of the Greyhound bus just as it was opening.

Her face was bright, her smile wide as the bus driver began to help the passengers down. "Watch your step, sir . . . . Have a nice day, ma'am." She shifted her weight impatiently, her eyes on the passengers. Her smile faded as the last passenger descended, and it was not Uncle Newt.

"Reckon he doesn't know to get off?" Mrs. Glory asked. She was walking the length of the bus now, peering up at the faces in the windows.

"He knows to get off," Mr. Glory said.

"Well, lots of times people in prison don't know how to do for themselves when they get out. They need help."

She came back on the other side of the bus. "I don't think he's on there."

Anna said to the driver, "My uncle was supposed to be on this bus."

"What does he look like?"

"Well, he's just kind of—" She paused. She wanted to put it as kindly as possible. "He's an average sort of man. He's—"

"I'll check," Mr. Glory said. He had suddenly remembered how, as a boy, Newt would occasionally hide on the floor of the car to avoid being kissed by relatives.

Mr. Glory boarded the bus and went down the aisle, looking on and under each seat like a policeman. Then he came back and stood in the doorway and looked down at his family.

"He's gone," he said.

Fugitive

"I wanted to see Uncle Newt," Joshua whined as the blue bus pulled away from the station.

"Me too."

"Watch out for that truck!" Mrs. Glory screamed.

Mr. Glory avoided the beer truck by slamming on the brakes. The whole family jammed into the seats in front of them.

"John!" Mrs. Glory said as she straightened.

Mr. Glory did not answer. He remained hunched over the steering wheel. After a moment he took a deep breath and restarted the engine.

Joshua pushed himself up by leaning hard on Matthew's back. Matthew came up with his fists raised, but Joshua was already looking innocently out the window.

Joshua was still hoping to catch a glimpse of Uncle Newt, to cry, "I see him!" It was always a triumph to see something before Matthew did. Their rides to singing engagements were spent yelling, "I see the river!", yelling back, "I saw it before you!"

"Where do you think Uncle Newt could be?" Anna asked. She was not on the back seat where she usually sat, but up front with the family.

"Did you hear what the bus driver said about the man who got off in Spartanburg? That was Newt, don't you think, John?"

Mr. Glory did not answer. With a jerk of his shoulders he threw the bus into third gear.

Mrs. Glory said, "It sounds like him—bolting off the bus, spilling people's things, running away. Newt never could face up to anything. He'd run like a scared rabbit if you looked at him."

"But why would he run from me—us?" Anna asked. The thought was unexpectedly painful. "Mom, maybe we should drive to Spartanburg—"

"And do what, Anna? Drive up and down the streets looking for a man we might not even recognize?"

"I'd know him," Joshua said, leaning forward. "He's going to be real pale, and his clothes won't fit right, and he'll—"

"The last time I saw Newt," Mrs. Glory said, interrupting, "was eight years ago at a family reunion, a picnic. Well, I wanted to be nice and so I went over to hug Newt—everybody was hugging everybody else—and he jumped back like I had a disease. I never will forget the look on his face when he saw me coming."

"Did you hug him anyway?" Matthew asked. He didn't care for affectionate relatives himself.

"I had to. I already had my arms out. And Newt cringed and ducked his head—he did everything but dig a hole in the ground and disappear."

Mrs. Glory puffed up her beehive hairdo. The memory still stung. "Later Cousin Annabelle said, 'Didn't you know? Newt can't stand to be hugged.' And I said, 'Anybody that can't stand to be hugged doesn't belong at a family reunion.' "

"Mom, you and Dad would recognize him," Anna said.

"It's been eight years. I told your father this morning he'd probably have to point Newt out to me."

"Well, we ought to do *something*."

"I look at it this way. If Newt doesn't want to come, if he doesn't want to be part of our family, if he wants to get away from us so bad that he'll knock people down getting off a bus—well, that's fine with me."

"Maybe he's—I don't know—real shy. Maybe . . ." Anna leaned back in her seat. Suddenly she could imagine Uncle Newt sitting on the Greyhound bus, alone, looking out the window, riding away from prison and toward a

50

family he hardly knew. She could imagine the bus driver saying, "Next stop Greenville," could imagine the panic that would grab Uncle Newt and send him dashing down the aisle and out into the open air.

It was odd. A week ago Anna's English teacher had asked the class to imagine that they were someone else and to write a composition about it. Anna had sat there, staring at her blank paper, while around her students scribbled away, pretending to be Howard Cosell, Barbara Walters, Nancy Reagan. The trouble was Anna could not imagine what it would be like to be somebody else.

And yet now, without even trying, she had done it. She had, for a moment, become Uncle Newt charging down the aisle, jumping to the ground, running through the streets of Spartanburg, his overcoat flapping behind him, his suitcase slapping against his leg.

"Newt never was one of my favorite people," Mrs. Glory said, as if that were the end of the matter.

"Mom!"

"Well, he wasn't, and if he keeps on acting this way, Anna, running like a fugitive, they'll take him back to prison. He's supposed to settle down somewhere."

"Is that true? Dad, would they make him go back?"

"I'm driving," Mr. Glory snapped.

"Dad—"

"Don't bother your father when he's driving." Mrs. Glory did not want any more distractions. Her knees still hurt from the beer truck incident.

"But I couldn't stand it if Uncle Newt went back to prison. I really couldn't."

"Don't get so emotional, Anna. You've never even seen the man."

"I must have. I was at the picnic. I—" She touched her father on the shoulder. "Dad, you've got to turn around."

Mrs. Glory reached out quickly and batted Anna's arm away. Her look at Anna was such a warning that Anna got up and, holding onto the seats, moved to the rear of the bus.

"If he does have to go back to prison," Joshua commented, "I hope it's before I finish my report so—"

Anna, passing him, let her hand fall on his shoulder. She squeezed it hard enough to make him say, "Ow."

Angel turned around. Her blue eyes seemed to look beyond Anna. "We'll see him soon, Anna," she said in her soft prophetic voice.

Anna sat on the last seat with a sigh, and the Glory family rode the rest of the way home with only the rattling and backfiring of the bus to break the silence.

The
Autographs

Joshua and Matthew were waiting to go up onto the stage
of the Central High Auditorium. They had on their blue
outfits, and Joshua had a blue scarf tied around his head,
Indian style, to hide his stitches.

Joshua was pleased with the way the scarf looked and
with the fact that Matthew didn't have one. He was standing there, imagining how he looked to the audience, when
two girls came up.

"She wants your autograph," one said.

"Mine?" He glanced around to see if, perhaps, someone famous was standing behind him. He had not thought
he looked *that* good.

"*I* don't want his autograph. *You* want it. *She's* the one wants it.

"I don't! She wants it. She says you're good-looking."

"*You* said he was good-looking."

As the girls argued pleasantly about which one wanted the autograph, Joshua said, "You can both have one."

He took the scrap of notebook paper, tore it carefully in half. "I don't have anything to lean on." These were his first autographs, and he wanted to do it right.

"Lean on my back," the fat girl said quickly.

"Well, all right." He would rather have leaned on the redhead's back, but she didn't offer it. He signed the pieces of paper slowly and carefully. Twice the ball-point pen poked through the paper and left small blue dots on the fat girl's blouse. "Excuse me," he said each time.

"There." He handed the small soiled scraps of paper to the girls. For the first time in his life he wished he had followed his mother's orders and washed his hands.

At that moment, the greatest personal triumph of his life, Matthew stepped in and said, "You can have my autograph too."

"He's nobody," Joshua told them quickly. "Just my brother."

He elbowed Matthew out of the way and kept him there. When Matthew tried to pass him on the right, he stepped to the right. When Matthew tried to pass him on the left, he was there too. He had done this with great skill four times when he heard their introduction. "Ladies and gentlemen, it's my pleasure to present to you the *Glory Gospel Singers!*"

"I've got to go. That's me," Joshua said.

Turning, he shoved Matthew up the steps ahead of him. Matthew stumbled and Joshua passed him without a glance.

The applause was building. As Joshua moved into the lights, he knew at last what it was like to be a star. He felt taller, better-looking.

He sat at his drums and watched the two girls going down the aisle, the scraps of paper held like tickets between their fingers. They took seats in the third row. Joshua made a mental note to keep an eye on them and to add extra beats and flourishes when they were watching.

"I'll get you for that," Matthew muttered as he got into place.

"Go ahead and try," he answered back.

It was halfway through the program, and Mr. Glory was at the front of the stage, leaning forward. His handsome face was shining with sweat.

The faces looking back at him were dull, without expression. A woman in the second row had fallen asleep. Things weren't going well.

"Now, boys and girls, I want to tell you a little story about myself." Someone in the back of the auditorium groaned. "When I was a little boy going to Bible school, I was always having to learn the books of the Bible or the names of the prophets, but I never had to learn the apostles because my mama taught me their names a long time ago. I remember she'd sing . . ."

At a nod of his head, Mrs. Glory began an introduction that caused the upright piano to tremble, and the twins came down hard on their drums. Mr. Glory sang:

"Oh, let us name the apostles
Peter, Philip, John, Matthew,
Let us call their names out
Simon, Judas, Thomas, too.
Let us name them one by one
Till the roll is called and done.
Matthias! Jude! James! Andrew!
And Bar-tho-lo-mew!

"Let's sing it together, boys and girls. It starts 'Let us name the apostles.' Here we go."

At the back of the auditorium Anna was sitting with her eyes closed, slumped in her seat. She was waiting for the program to end so she could sell tapes and albums.

She could already tell that it was going to be a poor night for sales. The way the crowd was sitting, not clapping in time to the music, the kids not singing along—and when Mr. Glory had sung "Reach Up and Touch the Master," only three hands, other than his, had reached toward the dingy ceiling. Another bad sign. On a good night every arm in the audience would be raised, waving.

She slumped lower in her seat. Her father always seemed to hold her personally responsible when the sales were less

56

than twenty. "You didn't try," he'd say. She imitated the cold expression that came over his face, and then she opened her eyes and glanced quickly around to see if anyone had noticed.

"Come on, kids!" Mr. Glory shouted. He sounded tired. A few mothers, out of sympathy, nudged their children and said, "Sing."

"Now, we're going to have a contest."

There were groans throughout the audience at this.

"We're going to see who knows the most names of the apostles—the girls or the boys. Girls, I'll sing the first line and see if you can sing the second. 'Oh, let us name the apostles—' "

There was a jumble of names and laughter.

"Well, boys, I know you can do better than that. Here's the third line. 'Let us call their names out—' "

" 'Simon, Judas, Thomas too.' "

"That was better. 'Let us name them one by one till the roll is called and done.' Everybody."

" 'Matthias! Jude! James! Andrew! And Bar-tho-lo-mew!' "

"Let's do the whole thing now. All together. 'Oh, let us—' "

The outside door opened behind Anna, and she heard the sound of rain. That was another bad sign, she thought glumly. People would not buy records because they would be in a hurry to get home.

She glanced around to see who had entered.

The
Man in
Gray

A man in a gray overcoat was standing in the doorway, looking down, shaking the rain from his coat. He watched the drops as they struck the floor, as if he had not been out in the rain often, as if what he was doing were a novelty.

Anna decided not to ask him if he had a ticket. The performance was almost over—just one more song, so it didn't matter.

Anyway, the man did not seem interested in sitting down. He was standing back in the shadows, his eyes looking at the floor. His hat was in his hands in an old-timey gesture of politeness. He had probably come in to get out of the rain, Anna decided, or to give somebody a ride home. She turned back to the stage.

Mr. Glory had finished the singing contest—an obvious relief to everyone—and was now standing back as Angel did her solo. Then he stepped up to the mike and began his spiel about the records and albums. "And on these records and cassette tapes," he was saying, "are the greatest of the great, the most popular songs we've ever sung, and I know you'll want to get one."

Anna stood up and moved into the light.

"At the back of the auditorium one of the Glory girls, our little Anna—she can't sing, but ain't she pretty?—she'll be waiting to help you with your purchases. Hold up your hand, darling, so they can see where you're at."

Dutifully Anna held up her hand and then moved back out of the light. She bumped directly into the man who had moved into the doorway. She could smell the wet wool of his coat.

"Oh, I'm sorry. Excuse me."

"My fault." The man stepped back quickly with a slight bow. He moved out of the bright light.

Anna sat at the table and, ignoring the stranger, began to straighten the stacks of albums. She opened the cash box.

The man cleared his throat. "Are you one of the Glory family?"

"Yes."

"I thought so." Another pause. "You don't sing?"

"No."

"Don't that bother you?"

"Oh, it used to bother me sometimes, but I think I'm getting used to it. My grandmother used to say people could get used to anything. She used to say we could get used to hanging if we hung long enough."

"My mother used to say the same thing, but I sure do wonder sometimes."

"Me too."

He said quickly, "Anyway, you look like you know what you're doing. You probably sell a lot of them records."

"Sometimes I do. Tonight I probably won't. When it rains and when the kids don't join in the singing and people don't clap with the music—well, you can always tell when nobody's going to buy anything."

"I'll take one."

"Oh, you will? Great." Anna smiled. "What do you want—an album or a cassette tape?"

"It don't matter."

"Well, what do you have—a stereo or a tape player?"

"Neither one."

Anna really looked at the man for the first time. His face was round, and there was something childlike in his small, earnest smile. As she met his eyes, he looked away, embarrassed.

"Then what on earth do you want with one of these?"

He did not answer. His smile faded. Suddenly he looked as wet and uneasy as a stray dog.

"I mean, don't buy one just to be polite," she said.

"I won't—I wasn't—"

Anna smiled again. Her smile was gentler this time. "Listen, my father would be furious if he heard me say this, but save your money."

The man had taken out his wallet and was holding it open as if it were a small book he was going to read. "I would be glad to buy one."

"Well, thank you for that, but—"

"Really, I don't mind."

"No," Anna said firmly.

In the auditorium the music was swelling. The Glory family was singing the final bars of their theme song.

> *"If you sing*
> *With the Glorys*
> *Then you'll never,*
> *Never,*
> *Never,*
> *Sing a-lone!"*

"Good night, everybody," Mr. Glory shouted, "and may God bless you and keep you until we meet again."

"You'll have to excuse me," Anna said to the man. "People will be coming out now. I'll be too busy to talk."

"Of course." He folded his wallet and put it in his

pocket. Pulling back a little into his overcoat, he stepped back out of the way.

He's like a turtle, Anna thought, the way he retreats into his shell. "Get your Glory tapes and albums over here," she called as the people began filing out of the auditorium.

"Ma'am, would you like to—"

The people were pulling on their coats, hurrying for the door. They all made a point of not looking in Anna's direction.

"Ma'am, sir, would you—"

When the crowd had gone without buying one single tape and Anna looked up again, she saw that the man in the overcoat was no longer there.

It was then that she realized she had been talking to Uncle Newt.

In the Middle of Galaxians

"I want to play Ms. Pac Man."

"No, it's my quarter—I asked for it—and I'm playing Galaxians."

The Glory family had stopped to eat on the way home from their performance at the Central High Auditorium. Mr. and Mrs. Glory were sitting in a booth, tiredly leaning on their arms. Mr. Glory had not spoken since his final, "God bless you and keep you until we meet again."

Mr. Glory was depressed. In his mind he was blaming the rain, his wife's playing, and his children's singing for the dull, unsuccessful performance. Underneath was the nagging thought that he was the one who had not been at his best.

If that was true, he thought, it was because of Newt. Mr. Glory's brows lowered over his gray eyes.

His brother Newt had become like the bear in that old game they had once played as children. The bear would hide and the rest of them would go around the yard singing, "Ain't no bears out tonight, Papa killed them all last night." But they would know that the bear was there, somewhere in the dark bushes, waiting for the right moment to jump out and send them screaming for safety and the front porch.

Mr. Glory had been feeling Newt's presence for days. He even thought he had seen him driving past the house once in an old red Ford. That would have been like Newt, he thought, wanting to see without being seen, waiting for the worst possible moment—at a performance perhaps—to appear and ruin their lives.

"Here goes!" Joshua said.

He and Matthew were now in front of the Galaxians screen. Joshua dropped in his quarter and pushed the starting button. He always felt a chill of power when he started a video game. It was as if there really were an invasion and only he could stop it.

A burst of charge music came from the machine, and at the top of the screen purple and green and red invaders appeared in formation.

At the same time a lone spaceship, armed with a yellow

missile, appeared at the bottom. Joshua grasped the control and got set to fire. The bright invaders streaked toward Joshua's rocket, peeling off the top of the formation. Joshua dodged and fired, dodged and fired, gasping with pleasure as he made a hit. Then a red alien crashed into his spaceship and Matthew said quickly, "My turn."

With his left hand on the control, his right index finger on the firing button, Matthew began shooting. His smile grew tense. Galaxians was easy at first, but soon the aliens got quicker, shiftier, more threatening.

Joshua leaned over Matthew's shoulder, giving advice. By now whole invading parties were coming—red, purple, yellow. If a player was good enough to hit the yellow flagship, he got eight hundred extra points.

At a nearby table sat Anna and Angel. Anna was watching her brothers. Angel was gracefully shredding a paper napkin with her slender fingers.

Suddenly the door opened, a burst of cold damp air hit Anna's back, and she turned to see who had entered.

"Angel, that's him! There he is!" Anna turned back to her sister. "Remember I said I thought Uncle Newt came in at the end of the performance? Well, don't look now, but that's him!"

Angel lifted her head and looked directly at the man.

"Angel, I said not to look!" Anna ducked her head in embarrassment.

"Yes, that's Uncle Newt," Angel said. "I see him all the time."

"What do you mean—'all the time'?"

"Well, he was walking past our house two days ago. I usually don't notice people, but I remember him because when he saw me he ducked his head and walked away real fast. You know, like people do when they've done something wrong?"

"What else?"

"Yesterday he was parked in a car down the street, just sitting there like he was waiting for somebody. Only when he saw me, he started up the car, did a U-turn, and drove away."

Anna watched as Uncle Newt slid into a booth. He took off his hat and set it on the table. He kept his face turned to the window.

"Oh, here's the pizza," Angel said. "I just want the pepperoni." She pushed the napkin shreds aside so the waitress could set the pizza in front of her.

Anna was still looking at Uncle Newt. His head was lowered, his face hidden now behind the menu.

"Did you say anything to Dad about seeing Uncle Newt?"

"To Dad? Are you kidding? With the mood he's in?" Angel selected a piece of pepperoni and took a bite.

Anna glanced over at her father. He was angrily spearing his spaghetti, using his fork the way a farmer used a pitchfork. Mrs. Glory called, "Joshua, Matthew, the food's here."

There was no answer. Both boys were bent forward, hunched toward the video screen, intent. Whole invading parties were swarming. The screen lit up as Joshua, firing steadily, dropped a yellow invader. *Whoosh . . . kabam . . .* he fired, ducked, fired, and then scooted to the side of the screen, but a purple alien collided with his ship and the game was over.

Matthew's shoulders sagged. "Ask Mom for another quarter."

"You ask her. I asked the last time."

"Boys," Mrs. Glory called. "Come on. The food's getting cold."

"We're coming," Matthew called back. He was still holding on to the control. "You know what somebody at school told me? He said there's a game called Berserk, and when you go up to it, it says, 'Coin—detected—in—pocket.' It talks to you."

"I tell you what I like to play—Frogger. You have to get these frogs across the highway without getting squashed, and then you have to cross a river—you jump on logs and turtles—and then—"

"Boys!"

It was Mr. Glory this time. Everybody in the restaurant glanced up. "We're coming," Joshua said. The twins crossed the restaurant so quickly they slammed into each other getting into the booth.

"I wonder if Dad's seen Uncle Newt sitting over there," Anna said to Angel.

Angel reached for another pepperoni. "If he had, we'd know it," she said.

The
Incident
at the
Pizza Parlor

"You girls from around here?"

Anna looked up, startled. She had been so intent on watching Uncle Newt that she had not noticed the two boys approaching their table.

One boy was standing back, looking at the floor. The other was grinning at Angel, scratching his chest through his plastic jacket, as if he were strumming a guitar.

Anna did not bother to answer. She looked across the room at Uncle Newt. The waitress was at his table, taking his order. Uncle Newt had spoken so softly that the waitress had to lean down to hear what he wanted.

"Just coffee?" she asked, straightening.

Uncle Newt nodded and looked out the window.

Ever since Anna had seen Uncle Newt come in, she had been trying to decide what to do. She knew he had come into the pizza parlor knowing they were there, yet now he was acting as if he did not want to be seen.

"What do you think?" Anna asked Angel. "Should I go over or—"

"Where are you from? You look familiar." The boy touched Angel's shoulder to get her attention.

"Look, we're trying to eat," Anna said coldly. She was used to handling this situation. Boys were always trying to meet Angel. Sometimes Anna felt like Angel's bodyguard, only these two couldn't have appeared at a worse time.

"You look lonesome, like you could use some company."

"Well, we couldn't."

"I'm not talking to you." He tugged a lock of Angel's long hair. "You're the one looks lonesome."

"We are trying to *eat*." Anna glanced over her shoulder at her father. He was bent over his spaghetti, scrowling. "Leave us alone."

Sometimes the boys who wanted to meet Angel were funny. One time in Belton a boy had pretended to be Hungarian and had gotten another boy to pretend to translate, but these boys weren't funny. There was something almost threatening about the way the one in the plastic jacket was pressing against Angel's chair.

69

"Mind if I sit down?"

"Yes!"

The boy pulled out the chair next to Angel's and snaked his hips onto the seat. He unzipped his plastic jacket and strummed his chest. "Aren't you a cheerleader from Central High?"

"Look, will you get out of that chair and leave us alone?"

As Anna spoke, she glanced over at Uncle Newt's booth. He was watching what was happening at their table, but when he saw Anna looking at him, he ducked his head. He stared intently at the napkin and spoon the waitress had brought him.

Angel put a piece of pepperoni into her mouth. She licked her fingers. She did not seem to be aware that anything disturbing was going on.

"Listen, that is our father over there in the third booth," Anna said, "and he does not allow us to talk to strange boys."

"Yeah, that's your father, and that fat lady with him is my Aunt Bessie."

"I'm serious. I—"

"Look, I'm trying to talk to your friend, all right? You talk to Monk. Monk, sit down here and talk to the girl."

"Come on," Monk said uneasily. "Let's get out of here."

"Monk, the girl is lonesome. Look at her. She—"

His words were cut off by the sound of chairs being

70

pushed aside. Monk looked up and stepped back. The boy in the plastic jacket threw back his head in time to see Mr. Glory crossing the restaurant, his face twisted with fury.

The boy made an effort to get up, but Mr. Glory got there first. He yanked the boy to his feet. The chair fell backward, and the boy's feet churned the air, trying to get back on the floor.

"What do you think you're doing?" Mr. Glory's face burned. His voice choked with fury. His hands shook with a killing rage.

The boy tried to speak, but Mr. Glory had twisted his jacket into a noose.

Monk stepped out of the way. His hands were lifted to show that he had no part in the dispute. He backed into a chair and then, on second thought, picked it up and held it in front of him, ready to use it like a lion tamer.

"You punks stay away from my daughter!"

There was such fury, such intensity in Mr. Glory that the boy stuttered. "I'm s-sorry. I—look, I—" He regained his footing. He twisted free from Mr. Glory's hand. "L-look, I thought I knew her, all right?" He pulled at his crumpled jacket. "We thought she was a cheerleader from Central, didn't we, Monk?"

Monk shrugged, keeping the chair carefully in front of him.

Mr. Glory looked closer at the boy. "Aren't you the same punks who—"

"Dad, that was over in Conway," Anna interrupted quickly.

"They look the same." All boys who were after Angel looked the same to Mr. Glory. He turned to Anna. "You could have prevented this. I think you enjoy—"

"I couldn't—I don't—"

"You know my feelings about boys."

"I asked them not to sit down, didn't I, Angel? I told them. I—"

"We're going!"

"I haven't eaten anything yet. I—"

"I'm through," Angel said, getting to her feet. All the pepperoni was gone.

"Maudine! Boys! We're leaving!"

"I haven't had one single bite!" Anna protested.

"Bring it along," her mother said quickly as she passed.

Anna began slapping pieces of pizza onto a napkin. Her head twisted in Uncle Newt's direction in a look of helpless anguish. Behind Anna, the boy zipped up his jacket and stuck his hands in his pockets.

"Is your old man crazy or what?"

Anna shrugged.

"He ought to be careful who he goes around calling punks, right, Monk?"

"It's over. Let it go," Monk answered.

Now that the boy was no longer in danger, his voice rose with a fury of his own. "Nobody calls me a punk. I

72

don't like being pushed around. You know that. I don't let anybody push me around.''

"He's crazy, man, don't fool with anybody crazy.''

"We're leaving!'' Mr. Glory announced, slapping money down on the counter. He took two steps and slammed the door shut behind him.

Holding the pizza in both hands, Anna crossed the hushed restaurant. She was determined to speak to Uncle Newt before she left. She got to his booth at the same time as the waitress.

The waitress said, "Here's your coffee—black.'' She set a mug before Uncle Newt, and he stared intently at the dark steaming liquid. He seemed to know that Anna was waiting behind the waitress.

"Uncle Newt!''

Still he did not look at her.

"Uncle Newt!''

"Anna!'' It was Mrs. Glory, sticking her head back in the door. "Your father's starting the bus! He's leaving!''

Anna heard the backfire of the engine. She said again, "Uncle Newt!''

As the waitress stepped out of the way, he looked up. He squinted, as if he were looking into a light that was too bright.

"I'm Anna.'' She smiled nervously. "I just had to say hello. I—''

"*Anna!*''

"You better go."

"Yes . . . good-bye."

She ran for the door and crossed the graveled parking lot in the rain. She got to the bus as Mr. Glory closed the door. She beat on it. Glaring down at her, he snapped it open and Anna climbed in.

She stumbled onto the front seat, and her pizza hit the floor with a splat. "I'll get it," Mrs. Glory said quickly. "It's not ruined. I can brush it off."

"I don't want it any more," Anna said.

Holding onto the seats, she made her way to the last seat on the bus. She wiped a clear circle in the mist on the window and looked at the restaurant.

Inside, the two boys were still standing by the table, arguing. The one in the plastic jacket was pointing at the bus, his finger jabbing angrily at the air.

With a crunch of gravel the bus jerked into motion. In a wide arc it turned onto Rockford Road.

Anna kept her face to the window. In the rosy glow of the neon sign, she could see the round oval of Uncle Newt's face watching them as they drove away.

Followed!

Anna sat on the last seat of the bus, staring out the window. She was watching for car lights on the road behind, but the road remained dark and empty. Only one truck had passed since they left the pizza parlor.

Rockford Road was a long stretch of worn blacktop that was not heavily traveled. On one side ran Sugar Creek, a stream that overflowed its banks regularly; on the other, a steep bank of rock. The white center line had not been painted in years.

Anna dropped her face onto her arm. She knew now that Uncle Newt was not going to follow them. She felt she would never see him again. She had scared him off by rushing over to him in the restaurant, and that was the last thing she had wanted to do.

The rain was coming down harder now. It washed back over the bus in sheets, and the wind rattled the old windows.

Anna did not notice the noise. She was going over her meeting with Uncle Newt. Again and again she repeated in her mind what she had said. "I'm Anna. I just had to say hello," and then he said, "You better go," and then she said, "Good-bye." That was all. She sighed with dissatisfaction.

If those stupid boys hadn't come up, she thought as she stared with slitted eyes at the long stretch of dark road behind them. If that boy in the plastic jacket hadn't sat down beside Angel and—

"John!" Mrs. Glory cried out in the front of the bus. Her voice was sharp with concern. The Glory bus had started to shimmy when it hit forty miles an hour, and this scared her.

"You want to drive?" Mr. Glory did not take his Pall Mall from between his teeth or look at her.

"No, but—"

"Then shut up."

"But the shaking . . . and . . . the windshield wipers." She was unable to remain silent, yet afraid to say anything more.

It seemed to her that nothing was right with the bus

tonight. Not only was it shaking in a terrible way, but the windshield wipers didn't seem to have enough power to push the heavy rain away. The click of the blades was getting slower and slower. If the blades stopped . . . She clutched the ruined pizza tighter.

Mrs. Glory watched her husband anxiously. He was leaning forward over the steering wheel, peering through the sheets of rain. His back was tense, his shoulders hunched. He puffed constantly on his cigarette. Mrs. Glory had the feeling that if it hadn't been for the faint white line down the center of the road, they would already have been in the ditch.

"Please don't go so fast, Dad," Angel asked from the third seat. "It makes me sick after I've eaten." It was so unusual for Angel to say anything about his driving that Mr. Glory slowed down slightly.

The trembling of the bus stopped, and Mrs. Glory looked around gratefully at her older daughter. "Thank you," she mouthed as she turned back to watch the road ahead. The pizza in her lap dropped to the floor again, this time un-noticed.

On the back seat Anna had heard her father's sharp re-tort. Her father was so different now from the way he was onstage. She knew how hard he worked on his stage ap-pearance—Grecian comb to turn his hair black again, makeup to hide the bags under his eyes, scarves to hide his sagging neck.

But when he leaned so close to the mike that the audi-

77

ence could hear him breathing, and when he said in that low, sincere voice, "And now it's hymn time, and tonight we would like to do my grandaddy's favorite, 'The Old Rugged Cross,' " Anna would forget all that. She would believe with the audience in his absolute goodness.

She turned back to the empty road that stretched behind the bus. She was more worried about Uncle Newt than about her father's driving. Where would he go now? What was he going to do?

The Glory bus rounded a curve, veered over the white center line, and Mr. Glory brought it back with a sharp spin of the steering wheel. At that moment the windshield wipers stopped completely.

Mrs. Glory gasped and folded her hands beneath her chin in prayer. She closed her eyes. As she waited, she heard the labored click as the windshield wipers started up again. Her sigh trembled with relief. She opened her eyes to watch for the next crisis.

On the fourth seat of the Glory bus Matthew was curled up with his eyes closed. He was passing the time by planning revenge on Joshua. All evening, even when they had been sharing the game of Galaxians, revenge had been in the back of his mind. Now he was giving the matter his full attention.

This particular revenge had to be something special, he told himself. He couldn't just pretend to lose balance and fall on him or something. It had to be *right*. Matthew was particular about his acts of vengeance.

As he lay there, listening to the rain, he began to go over the incident again. He remembered Joshua pushing him out of the way, saying, "He's nobody. Just my brother." Nobody! That wasn't fair. He had as much right as Joshua to sign autographs. And the girls—well, there had been two of them. Joshua could have shared.

Suddenly he noticed a movement across the aisle. Joshua was scratching his stitches, something he had been forbidden to do. "You are not to touch those stitches," he had been told at least a hundred times.

"Mom, Joshua's scratching his stitches," Matthew sang out happily.

"I'm not scratching them," Joshua protested. "I'm scratching *around* them."

"Huh-uh! I saw him. He was scratching his stitches."

"You boys be quiet."

Mrs. Glory turned and swatted the only twin she could reach—Matthew.

Matthew scrambled up in his seat. "That's not fair! He scratches his stitches and I get hit!"

A second swat silenced him. Now, he thought darkly as he settled down again, he would have to have *double* revenge.

At the back of the bus Anna straightened. She could see car lights in the distance. She widened the clear circle on the window.

It was Uncle Newt! She had not scared him away, after all. Anna leaned her chin on her arm and watched, smiling, as the wavering car lights came closer.

Danger
from
Behind

A silence had fallen inside the Glory bus. Both Mr. and Mrs. Glory were tensely watching the road ahead through the faulty windshield wipers. Angel was twisting her hair around her fingers, her eyes closed, her head laid back. The twins had fallen asleep on opposite seats, curled forward in identical positions. Anna was looking out the back window.

For the past five minutes Anna had been watching the car lights coming closer. She had now begun to wonder if it really could be Uncle Newt's car. She had the feeling that Uncle Newt would have stayed back, merely kept the bus in sight. This car was moving steadily closer.

Anna got up. Holding onto the seats, she made her way forward. She slipped into the seat opposite Angel. "Angel?"

"What?" Angel did not open her eyes.

"What did Uncle Newt's car look like?"

"Ancient."

"Anything else?"

"Rusty, junky, falling apart. The first time I saw it I thought it had been abandoned. Then I saw him behind the wheel."

"Oh. Thanks."

Anna went back to the window. The car was even closer now. In the glow of the headlights she could see the sleek hood, the high chrome bumper, the smooth paint. "It's not him," she said to herself.

She raised her eyes. Farther back on the road, she saw the lights of another car, but Anna didn't have much hope that that would be Uncle Newt either. She leaned her head against her arms and closed her eyes.

The rocking movement of the bus was putting her to sleep when a light in her face startled her. She opened her eyes.

The car was directly behind the bus now. Anna straightened. She thought at first that the car was going to pass, but it was too close. She leaned against the glass for a better view. At that moment she recognized the boy in the plastic jacket. He was beside the driver, leaning forward, grinning up at the bus. His drooping eyelids made slits of his eyes. He turned to the driver, said something, laughed.

For a moment Anna froze. There was something sinister about the boy's expression. She remembered the look in his eyes at the restaurant, the anger in his voice as he had said, "Nobody calls me a punk."

She got up. Swaying, she made her way quickly up the aisle. "Dad?"

"Don't bother your father," Mrs. Glory said in a strained voice. The windshield wipers were acting up again. Each time they slowed, her pulse quickened.

Mr. Glory did not look around. He was lighting another cigarette from the one he had just finished smoking.

Anna sat down in the seat behind him. "Dad, those guys are behind us."

"What guys, Anna?" Mrs. Glory asked. Anna had her attention at last.

"The ones in the restaurant. You know, Mom, the ones who came over to our table, the ones Dad yelled at?"

"Did you hear that, John?" Mrs. Glory leaned across the aisle anxiously. Her round knees punched into the opposite seat.

"I heard."

"Dad, I think they're going to try something."

"What, Anna?" Mrs. Glory asked.

"I don't know—force us off the road or something. They're too close."

Mr. Glory's eyes darted to the rearview mirror to check

the headlights of the car behind. Then he stepped on the gas. Mrs. Glory clasped her hands over her heart as the bus began to shimmy. Danger was everywhere now—in the sluggish windshield wipers, the boys behind them, the trembling bus. "Please, John," she moaned.

"Please what? Please let those punks run us off the road?"

"We don't know that's what they're going to do. Maybe they're in a hurry. Maybe they want to pass."

"They can pass if they want to," Mr. Glory snapped. "They have room."

"John, they don't. Slow down and move over a little. Please!"

With his lips clamped on his cigarette, Mr. Glory glanced down at the speedometer. He eased up on the gas pedal. Forty-five . . . forty . . . thirty-five . . . thirty . . .

Anna glanced from the speedometer to the back of the bus where the lights of the other car lit up the window.

"If they wanted to pass," Mr. Glory said beneath his breath, "they'd pass. Pass, you punks!"

"What's happening?" Joshua asked, rising from his sleeping position. "What's going on?"

"Nothing," Anna said. "Just some boys trying to be funny."

"What are they doing?"

"Nothing, just—"

Joshua scrambled down the aisle and looked out the back

window. "It's a Thunderbird," he called. He knew cars. His voice rose. "And it's getting ready to bump into us!"

At that moment the Glorys felt the jarring thud as the car struck the back of the bus.

The
Rockford
Accident

The jolt flung the Glorys forward and then backward in their seats. Angel's eyes snapped open. Matthew awoke as he hit the seat in front of him. The sound of Mrs. Glory's sharp scream hung in the air long after they had recovered.

"John, pull over," Mrs. Glory said then in a soft, pleading voice, her hands again over her heart. "Stop. Let them pass."

Mr. Glory did not answer. His eyes darted from the rearview mirror to the road ahead.

"What's happening now?" Anna called back to Joshua.

He was at the window again, his forehead against the cold glass.

"Nothing," he reported. "The Thunderbird's still there, and it's not slowing down. They're blowing the horn!" His last words were lost in the long, arrogant blast of the car's horn.

"John, *please!*"

At the wheel of the Glory bus, Mr. Glory started to tremble. This was something he had never been able to control. All his life the combination of helplessness and fear had caused his bones to rattle. As a boy his nickname had been "Shaky."

"John!" Mrs. Glory cried sharply. She moved to the edge of her seat. She felt she had lost her husband's attention. He seemed to be in a trance. "John!"

"He's coming at us again!" Joshua called.

The Glory family tensed. Anna braced herself against the back of her father's seat. Her knuckles were white.

"Hold on," Mrs. Glory cried.

The jolt came then, hard. Anna's head was flung against her father's seat. She heard her mother scream, heard Joshua yell as he was thrown backward into the aisle. She straightened. In the pale light from the dashboard her eyes were wide with her own fear.

She wet her dry lips. "Maybe we *should* pull over, Dad."

Anna put her hand on her father's shoulder as she spoke,

and she felt him trembling. It was as frightening as feeling stone tremble. "Dad?" She had never thought of her father as anything but hard and unyielding. She said again, "Dad?"

Mr. Glory did not answer. His shoulder jerked as he reached down to shift gears, again as he clutched the steering wheel. And beneath was the terrible shivering, as if his very bones had turned to ice. Anna was more alarmed by this than she was by the boys behind them.

"Dad, are you all right?"

As she leaned forward, waiting for his answer, Joshua screamed, "He's coming at us again!"

Instantly Mr. Glory steered the bus to the right in a desperate attempt to avoid the jolt. Anna was thrown sideways. Behind them, tires screeched.

"That stopped them," Joshua yelled in triumph. "They missed!"

"For *now*," Matthew added. Both boys were at the back of the bus now, peering with white faces at the car behind them.

"I don't believe this," Matthew added. "Why doesn't he leave us alone?"

Joshua said, "I told you we needed a CB. We could call the police!" Joshua was holding onto the seat with both hands now, swaying as wildly as if he were riding a bucking horse.

"He's coming again!"

"Dad, he's coming!"

88

Mr. Glory strained forward. His shoulders flexed as he steered to the right again. This time he went too far. Anna felt the front wheel slip off the crumbling blacktop and onto the soft earth. Mr. Glory yanked the wheel to the left.

The bus wavered on the edge of the road, swerving back and forth. The headlights shone first on the trees to the left, then on the stone bank on the right. The Thunderbird passed, sending a spray of water up onto the windshield.

At that moment the windshield wipers stopped. Mr. Glory peered blindly over the steering wheel. The world was lost in a sheet of water. He hit the brake. For what seemed an eternity the bus wavered.

Anna, with her hand on her father's shoulder, knew the exact moment when her father lost control of the bus. He was pulling the steering wheel to the left with all his strength, and the bus turned to the right.

Anna gasped as the bus went completely off the road. A flash of lightning lit up the world, and Anna saw trees looming ahead.

For a moment the top-heavy bus swayed in the soft earth. Mr. Glory clung to the useless steering wheel, braced for the crash.

Before Anna buried her head in her arms, the windshield wipers swept across the windshield for one last time, and Anna saw the trees directly ahead. She held on for dear life.

Overturned

The head-on crash Anna expected did not happen. At the last moment the bus ground-looped. Skidding in the soft, slick earth, it hit the trees sideways.

There was the awful sound of metal scraping against wood, and a pause. Then, with a terrible slowness, like a prehistoric animal dying, the Glory bus turned over onto its side. It rested against trees, which bent beneath the weight.

The shock jarred Anna from her seat. She plunged across the bus and landed against the opposite window, her shoulder jammed into the cold glass. Drums overturned and crashed against the side of the bus. People screamed.

Then Anna was aware only of the sound of the bus motor, still running, of tires spinning uselessly in the air. The noises gave her a strange, almost safe feeling, as if the bus were trying to straighten itself and drive on as before.

Anna raised her head. The headlights from the Thunderbird were shining on the bus now, and in that light Anna could see her mother beside her. Beyond, Angel was trying to sit up, and her father, somehow still suspended in the driver's seat, was struggling to free himself.

In the back of the bus one of the twins called, "Help!" The other, upside down, called a weaker, "Me, too!"

Leaning forward, Anna heard the screech of tires as the Thunderbird drove away. The sound of the engine faded away in the distance. The light was gone with it, and the Glorys were left with only the dim glow from the dashboard.

"Kids?" Mrs. Glory called. Her weak voice was almost lost in the sound of the racing bus engine. The engine was running stronger now than it had ever done on the road.

"I'm all right," Anna answered. "I'm right beside you."

"Angel?"

"I'm all right."

"Boys?"

Before the twins could answer, one of the trees that the bus was leaning against snapped. The sound was as sharp as gunfire. The front of the bus dipped alarmingly. Then there was another crack. A second tree bent and broke.

Anna's hands flew up as she felt the bus sliding over the embankment to the creek below. She screamed. She tumbled backward.

The bus thudded onto its top. It slid, hit a tree, hesitated for a moment, and rolled over again. Then it began its drop down the long steep bank.

Anna's body was being battered around the inside of the bus as if she were a toy. She screamed as she was slammed into the side of the bus. She struck a seat, felt another body fall against her back. She struck metal, glass, bit through her lip as her face smashed into the floor.

She screamed again and again. She heard other screams, too, but these human sounds became lost in the terrible metallic groans of the bus as it slammed down the rugged bank.

Nothing could stop it. It crashed into rocks. It flattened brush. It tore the limbs off trees. It turned over again.

Then there was one last earsplitting splash, followed by a moment that sounded like silence because the only noise was that of water against the bus.

The Glory bus had come to rest in the creek. It was upside down. The front of the bus was slowly sinking into the rain-swollen waters; the back was in the air. The whole thing seemed about to go underwater at any moment.

The current rushed around the bus. The bus was lifted for a moment and carried forward. It came to rest jammed against some rocks.

Inside the bus Anna lay where she had fallen. She was

92

in the front corner of the bus, crumpled on her side. She opened her eyes.

She could not see anything. The darkness was absolute. Anna blinked, waiting for her eyes to adjust. The darkness continued. There was not even the memory of light.

It was like the time Anna had gone into a cave. The Glorys had been on their way home from a performance in Virginia and, on the twins' urging, they had stopped at Endless Caverns.

Deep within the cave, the guide had cut off the lights for a moment. The darkness had been so awesome that everybody fell silent. No one moved. Even the twins, who had planned to play tricks on each other in the dark, were still standing stockstill when the lights came on again.

Anna put her hand to her eyes. Pain shot through her shoulder, and she dropped her hand limply to her side.

As she lay there, stunned, not sure where she was or what had happened, a streak of lightning jagged in the sky. It repeated itself, turning the world white with a light brighter than the sun.

Anna, her eyes wide with shock and fear, looked out on a world literally turned upside down. The seats of the bus were overhead. The lightning flashed beyond them. She lay on the ceiling. Darkness and, somehow, water were below.

The darkness came again, merciful this time. And Anna closed her eyes and drifted into unconsciousness.

Dark
Water

When Anna opened her eyes again, her body was still twisted into the same corner of the bus. She did not know where she was. She did not even remember that she had, five minutes before, opened her eyes and in a flash of lightning seen the upside-down world.

She stretched one trembling hand out into the darkness. She felt nothing familiar. The only sound was the rushing of water close by. There was nothing familiar in that, either.

Suddenly she heard someone moan. "Who's there?" she cried sharply.

There was no answer.

Anna shifted. She struggled to lift her head, and nausea swept over her. Her head throbbed. The taste of blood was in her mouth. Icy fingers wrapped around her ankles.

"Mom?" Anna reached out and touched slivers of broken glass. She rubbed her fingers over the glass, wondering what it was. She touched cloth. Her fingers curled around the fabric.

"Mom?"

It was not her mother, only one of the costumes, fallen from its hanger. It clung wetly to her hand.

The icy water was sweeping higher. It was above her ankles now. She shuddered with cold and pulled her feet out of the water. She paused and listened. Someone was moaning.

Anna crawled forward. She touched someone in the dark—and gasped. "Who's there?" Her teeth were chattering now. No answer. "Who are you?"

Anna ran her fingers over the still face. "Is that you, Mom?"

The icy water had risen about her feet again. As Anna tried to crawl out of it, lightning flashed and thunder boomed. The lightning turned the world white again, and Anna paused, frozen with horror.

She saw her surroundings then so vividly that the image would be burned into her brain forever. The upside-down bus. Her mother's still profile. Her father, suspended upside down in the driver's seat, his arms hanging over his head as if in surrender. The costumes on the dark water.

The body of Angel, her arm laid gracefully on the costumes, her long hair trailing into the water.

Then darkness came and Anna clawed her way forward. As she knelt over her mother's body, she suddenly heard a new sound, a rapping. It made no sense. "Mom, can you hear me?"

She thought she heard her mother speak. She bent her head closer. "Mom!"

It was then that she saw a light at the back of the bus. She looked up, squinting. A thin beam of light was shining around the inside of the bus, touching on the costumes, sliding over Angel's pale face, Mr. Glory's arms, then on her own face.

"Is someone there?" she asked, her voice cracking with fear and hope.

The small circle of light was turned backward to shine onto a round face. Anna blinked. The face seemed far away, something at the end of a long tunnel.

"It's me," a voice called. "It's Uncle Newt."

Anna knelt where she was. She watched as Uncle Newt crawled into the bus, the beam of his flashlight bouncing over the walls, the dripping seats. He came toward her, his feet sliding on the slick, wet ceiling.

"You all right?" He shone the light into her pale face. She nodded.

"Well, you're going to have to help me, honey. Can you move?"

Anna nodded again. Uncle Newt stuck his flashlight under one arm and helped her sit up.

"What happened?" she asked. "I can't remember anything."

"You had an accident. Some boys run you off the road. I knew what they were up to, but I couldn't stop them. Can you move your legs?"

"I think so. My feet are numb."

"By the time I caught up with you, the bus was off the road and them punks leaving. I got there to see you disappear down the bank."

Anna swayed, and Uncle Newt caught her around the shoulders. He said again, "You all right?"

"Yes."

"When I looked down the bank and saw where the bus was at—well, I thought you were goners."

"Where are we?"

"In the creek. The bus is upside down. That's why everything looks so strange, why the water is—" He broke off. "Right now we got to get you and your folks out of here."

"I can make it," Anna said. "You look after the others."

"The trouble is I need your help. Can you take your mother on this side?"

"I don't know—I—"

Anna lost her footing on the slick surface and went down on one knee. "Easy does it." Uncle Newt helped her up.

He bent over Mrs. Glory. "Maudine, it's Newt," he said in a loud voice. "You hear me, Maudine? We got to get you out of here."

Mrs. Glory moaned.

"She's coming to. Grab her under the arm and let's get going. Time's running out."

With a new urgency, forgetting her numb feet, her pain, Anna grabbed her mother's arm. She and Uncle Newt began moving Mrs. Glory toward the back door. Mrs. Glory moaned in protest, and her small shoeless feet trailed behind, twitching helplessly in the icy water.

At the door Uncle Newt said, "Hold your mother right there. Don't let her slip back while I climb outside. You got her?"

"Yes."

Anna was shuddering violently, her teeth clacking together so hard she could barely speak. There was a splash as Uncle Newt dropped into the water. Anna pressed against her mother, holding her by the door. Her eyes closed with the effort.

"All right, I'm ready!" Uncle Newt called.

"Come on, Mom."

Anna raised up slightly and, pulling her mother with her, leaned out the door. She hung there, too weak to move for a moment. The metal cut into her waist. "Uncle Newt?"

A bolt of lightning lit up the sky then, and Anna looked down with horror. Dark water swirled around the bus, rushing downstream with enough power to carry the whole bus with it.

"Let go. I've got her," Uncle Newt called in the darkness that followed.

The Rescue

Anna lay by the doorway, leaning her head against the metal frame. Her eyes were closed. She was startled when Uncle Newt took her by the shoulders and shook her. "Your brothers are over here, hon. Come on."

"Where are we?" she asked, looking around in confusion as the flashlight lit up the eerie scene.

Uncle Newt tugged her arm. "Come on. I got your mom to shore. She spoke. She said, 'Angel.' I reckon she— Here, give me a hand. Can you sit up, son?"

Joshua moaned, "No."

"Put your arm around me."

"I can't . . . I hurt."

Anna crawled toward them. She remembered now. She said, "We all hurt, Joshua, but we've got to get out or we're going to drown."

"Drown?"

"The water's rising, son." Uncle Newt slipped his arm under Joshua's shoulder. "The bus is braced against some rocks, and it's holding, but if the water gets higher . . ." His voice trailed off as he lifted Joshua. "Well, we're liable to wash on down to Columbia."

In the pale beam from the flashlight, Anna could see Matthew on the other side of Joshua. "I'll get him," she said, even though she was not sure she could. She grabbed Matthew's arm and began to drag him toward the door.

Matthew moaned. "He's alive," Anna told Uncle Newt.

"Here, I'll get them both at once. You just hold them while I get outside."

As Uncle Newt climbed back into the water, he said, "You take the light and see where the others are at."

"I know where they are."

"I'm ready," Uncle Newt called, and Anna thrust Joshua through the doorway.

"And here's Matthew." Anna shoved his limp body into Uncle Newt's arms. Then she picked up the light and shone it around the bus.

Angel lay where she had fallen, and Mr. Glory still hung upside down in the driver's seat. The water had risen to cover his hands now.

Anna crawled toward Angel, pushing objects aside as she moved. "Angel!" She knelt beside her. "Angel, wake up. We've got to get out of here. Angel, the bus is upside down in a river. We're going to drown if we don't get out!"

"Anna?" Angel whispered.

"Yes, it's me."

"I'm hurt."

"Everybody is."

"But I can't move. I'm—"

"I'll get her." It was Uncle Newt again. Anna shone the light on her sister. Her wet hair swung in a wide arc as Uncle Newt picked her up. Angel cried as he struggled to the door with her.

At the door Uncle Newt called, "Come on, Anna, you too."

"I have to help Dad."

"I'll help him. I want you out of here."

"I can't leave him!"

"Come on!"

In a daze Anna struggled to the door. Lightning flashed as she got there, and in the burst of light she climbed out and dropped into the cold water. She clung to the bus, gasping for breath, too weak to fight the current alone.

The lightning flashed again, and in the white world Anna saw Uncle Newt coming toward her. The water swirled around his chest now, and his round face was twisted with the effort. Overhead, the angry clouds rumbled. Then, just as Anna felt her hands slipping from the icy metal, Uncle Newt was there. He put his arm around her and carried her to the bank.

Anna felt herself being laid on the ground. Raindrops as big as marbles were falling on her face. She tried to lift her head.

Beside her, she could hear her sister crying and one of her brothers moaning. "I'm dying," he blubbered.

"Nobody's dy-dying," she stuttered.

"That's what it feels like."

Anna called, "Uncle Newt?"

Uncle Newt had gone back into the bus. The flashlight had died, and Uncle Newt was now searching in total darkness for his brother. He felt his way to the driver's seat, calling, "Bubba, Bubba," the name he had used when they were boys.

Suddenly the bus shifted, and Uncle Newt felt the water rise. He waited in a crouch until he was sure the bus was steady again. "Bubba!"

"I'm here."

Uncle Newt waded toward the weak sound of his brother's voice. "I'm stuck . . . trapped." Uncle Newt brushed against his brother's hand, which was trailing in the water. He reached out and held it. It was the first time the brothers had touched in thirteen years.

"What's holding you?" Uncle Newt asked, gasping, trembling from cold and desperation.

"It's my leg . . . the seat . . ."

Bracing against the side of the bus, Uncle Newt pulled on the metal seat. "It's giving a little." He strained with all his might. "Try to pull your leg out."

"I can't feel it any more. I—"

The bus shifted again as it was washed downstream by the current. The water rose in the bus. Uncle Newt held his breath until the bus came to rest against rocks.

A flash of lightning lit up the bus. Thunder roared. Uncle Newt saw his brother's face, now only inches above the water. "This is your last chance, Bubba," he gasped. "I'll pull on the seat, and you yank your leg out of there. You hear me?"

"I'll try . . . I don't—"

"Do it, Bubba. This is *it*!"

Uncle Newt braced his foot against the side of the bus and pulled on the twisted metal. He felt it loosen slightly. He strained harder, arching his whole body backward.

"*Now!*" he yelled.

There was a scream as Mr. Glory pulled his leg free. Mr. Glory tried to scramble out of his seat, but his leg was useless. He fell facedown in the water. He floundered, swallowed water, choked. Uncle Newt put his arm under his brother's shoulders and lifted him. Holding onto each other, they struggled to the door.

The water was flowing into the back of the bus now, filling it. Fighting the current and time and the weight of his brother, Uncle Newt lunged through the doorway. He plunged into the cold water for the last time. His head went under and then, as he bobbed up, his feet touched bottom for a moment.

Towing his brother behind him, he began to swim for shore.

The
Glory
Family

Anna remembered little of being carried up the bank on a stretcher or of her ride to the hospital in an ambulance. She heard nothing that was said to her, and the bright lights and the wailing siren had no meaning.

In the emergency room, however, with a doctor and nurse working over her, there had been one moment of absolute clarity. In all the confusion and urgency Anna had looked across the room and seen a familiar face in the doorway.

"Uncle Newt," she cried through teeth that were still chattering.

She had tried to raise her head. Hands pushed her back on the table.

"Anna," Uncle Newt called, somehow sensing what she wanted. "Everybody got out!" He lifted one hand, and Anna lay back, satisfied.

The next three days were a blur. Anna slept most of the time, drifting in and out of consciousness. Her first good morning came on Tuesday.

A nurse came into the room to take Anna's blood pressure and said, "Well, you're looking better today."

"Have I seen you before?" Anna asked.

"Every day."

"I don't remember." The nurse tightened the blood pressure cuff around Anna'a arm and pumped air into it.

"How's my family?" Anna asked.

"Let's see. Your sister had a compound fracture of the left arm, a broken collarbone, and bad bruises. Your mom—she must have good padding—she's just suffering from shock and exposure. Who else? Your dad's the worst—five broken ribs, a punctured lung, smashed left leg."

"And the twins?"

"Your brothers are driving everybody in Pediatrics crazy. Those boys are mean as snakes. They had a wheelchair race yesterday, almost ran over Dr. Perrini."

"They weren't hurt?"

"Cuts and bruises."

"Stitches?"

"No."

Anna smiled slightly. "I bet they were disappointed about that."

"Those boys are tough."

Anna's answer was cut off because the nurse put a thermometer in her mouth. When she could speak again, Anna asked, "Have you heard anything about my uncle?"

"Why, your uncle is a hero. He's been in all the headlines. 'Former Convict Rescues Family.' "

"I wish they hadn't said 'convict.' "

"No, something like that gives convicts a good name. The governor's talking about giving him a pardon."

"Really?"

"Yes, and something else good has come out of the accident. The town's taking up a collection for new costumes, new instruments, the works. They never did catch the boys who were responsible, but the town's behind you."

Anna rested against her pillow while the nurse made a note on her chart. "Has Uncle Newt been coming to the hospital?"

"One time. I didn't see him. Miss Hawkins was at the desk, and she said he came up, asked how you were, and after she told him you were all right, he left."

"He's shy."

The nurse stood at the foot of the bed, watching Anna. "You and your family were real lucky."

"I know that."

"I saved the newspapers for you. And when you see the pictures of the bus—that bus went all the way down Sugar Creek and crashed into the bridge. It was just a pile of twisted blue metal. When you see those pictures, you'll know how lucky you were."

"I know that now," Anna answered.

Outside Anna's room, in the hall, Mrs. Glory was beginning her morning rounds. She had a routine just like the nurses.

First she would check on Anna. Mrs. Glory had not worried about Anna, not even when the doctors told her it was touch and go. She knew Anna would pull through.

Then Mrs. Glory would go in to see her husband. He was in the men's ward at the end of the hall. When that was out of the way, she would stop in Angel's room.

Mrs. Glory was so glad that Angel's face had not been hurt. Angel was as beautiful as ever. It was a miracle. Her arms and legs were covered with cuts and scrapes. There was a bruise on her hip bigger than a grapefruit. But her face—Mrs. Glory considered this the hand of the Lord—was still perfect.

Mrs. Glory would linger in Angel's room, putting off as long as possible the moment when she had to go up to the fourth floor, Pediatrics. She dreaded that.

If the nurses up there told her one more time, "You've got to do something about the twins. They're driving us crazy." If they said that one more time, she would . . .

Mrs. Glory squared her plump shoulders under her bathrobe. She reminded herself that she would do nothing. She had promised, in that dark moment when the bus tipped over the bank and started down, that if her family was spared, she would never lose her temper again.

She went into Anna's room, smiling. Three days in the hospital had flattened her beehive hairdo so that she no longer looked like herself.

"Anna, you're awake!"

"Yes'm."

"You look fine."

"You too."

Mrs. Glory crossed to Anna's bed. In the new cheerful voice she had picked up from the nurses, she said, "Yes, we all look just fine."

Return Performance

The Glory family was on the stage of the George Washington High School auditorium. Mr. Glory was standing at the edge of the stage, leaning forward, talking to the audience.

"Friends, you all know how lucky the Glory family is to be here tonight. You read about our accident in the newspapers. We're just so grateful to be alive, to be up here onstage again, singing for you."

Mrs. Glory said, "Amen," from the piano bench.

"It's been like a miracle. And so tonight our first song is going to be 'We're Thankful,' because that's exactly what every one of us is. Maudine."

Mrs. Glory brought her small hands down on the bass notes and went up the keyboard, playing a series of chords that used every single note on the piano.

Mr. Glory stepped back. He walked with a limp—he always would—but tonight, for the first time, he felt no pain. His injury was forgotten in his happiness at being on the stage again.

> *Oh, we're thankful and we're grateful*
> *And we're singing His praise.*
> *We're telling everybody*
> *These are happy, happy days.*
> *He gave us our life*
> *Not once, but twice*
> *And we're thankful and we're grateful*
> *To the Lord.*
> *Oh, we're . . .*

In the back of the auditorium Anna sat watching her family on the stage. For this, their first performance since the accident, everything was new—new white outfits, new drums, new guitar. It did seem like a beginning.

There was a new feeling from the audience too. They had bought albums tonight even before the performance started. That had never happened before. Anna had already collected a hundred and twenty-eight dollars.

Anna glanced over her shoulder. Behind her the entrance was empty. Only the large white plaster statue of George Washington stood in the shadows.

112

In the two months since the Glorys' accident, Anna had been looking for Uncle Newt everywhere. She never went out of the house without searching for him, and she had not seen him once. It was as if he had disappeared from the earth.

"Where do you think Uncle Newt is?" she had asked her mother.

"He could be anywhere, Anna. He could be in Nome, Alaska, for all I know. Once he got his pardon, he was free to go anywhere."

"It looks like he would have called at least. Maybe something happened to him."

"I don't understand that man. I never have. I am as grateful to Newt as I've ever been to anybody in my life. We would all be dead if it wasn't for Newt. I said to your father, 'When I see that man I'm going to throw my arms around his neck and hug him to pieces.' Your father felt the same, in his own way. He told me he wanted Newt to sing with us, be one of the Glorys. Your father said, 'From now on, I'm treating Newt like a brother.' Only how are we going to do these things with him gone?"

"I guess you can't."

"Anybody else would *want* to be thanked. I just don't understand what gets into that man. It seems like he deliberately won't let people do what'll make them feel better. If I wasn't so grateful, I'd be downright mad."

"Now, Mom."

"I'm not mad," Mrs. Glory added quickly, remembering her promise. "It's just that when you owe somebody, you don't feel right until you've thanked them."

"It's like it's unfinished," Anna said.

"Exactly."

The fact that Anna had not seen her uncle since that moment in the recovery room did leave everything unfinished. Had that been his farewell, she wondered, that lifted hand in the doorway of the emergency room? It wasn't enough.

Angel had told her, "Quit looking for him. You're going to wear out your neck turning around so much."

"I can't help it, Angel," Anna had answered. "He's the only person I ever felt really close to."

Angel had looked at her with her pale eyes. "He's the only person you ever wanted to feel close to."

On the stage Mr. Glory was saying, "Thank you," to the audience. He adjusted the mike. "And now Angel is going to sing one of the songs her grandaddy wrote. This was the last song Grandaddy Glory wrote before he died, and the first time it was sung was at his funeral. 'I'm Almost over the Mountain, Going Home.' Angel."

Anna shifted in her seat. She watched as Angel, white flowers in her hair, came forward. The music began.

Audiences always got quieter when Angel sang, and tonight there was not a sound in the auditorium. As she listened, Anna thought that her family was better than before the accident. They were actually singing better.

Anna had noticed it for the first time in the hospital

when they had sung in the hall for the patients one afternoon. They had stood around Mr. Glory's wheelchair,
singing hymns together, and for the first time Anna had
been proud of them without being bitter that she wasn't
part of them.

Tonight her mother looked happier at the piano. Her
father's looks had softened. The twins looked the same,
and yet maybe they weren't after each other quite as hard
as before.

Suddenly Anna felt a cool breeze on the back of her
neck. Someone had opened the door in the entrance hall.

Anna wanted to turn around at once, but she stopped
herself. It might be Uncle Newt, she thought, as she had
thought many times in the past weeks. If it was, she did
not want to scare him off.

Onstage Angel was at the mike, singing the chorus.

> *"Yes, I'm almost over the mountain.*
> *Yes, I'm going home at last.*
> *Yes, I see the golden valley.*
> *I am almost to the pass."*

Anna was no longer listening to the music. The footsteps behind her were slow and reluctant, the way Uncle
Newt's would be, Anna thought. Anybody else would have
walked right over and looked in the auditorium to see who
was singing.

The footsteps stopped, and Anna turned her head.

115

The
Last
Good-bye

Uncle Newt was standing in the shadows by George Washington, dwarfed by the huge white statue. A baseball cap was in his hands. He was turning it around, smiling awkwardly.

Anna got up—she was smiling too—and walked toward him. They stepped back against the wall, farther away from the loud music. Anna said, "I was wondering if I was ever going to see you again."

"Well, here I am."

"I knew it was you when the door opened."

"Did you?"

116

There was a pause, and then Anna said in a rush, "The whole family's so proud of you. It's just—well, you're all we talk about these days."

"Well . . ." There was another pause. Uncle Newt glanced behind him at the door.

Anna went on in a rush. "They just want to thank you. That's all. And Dad wants you to sing with the family. He says you've got the best voice of any of the Glorys. And Mom wants you to live with us. She says—"

He shook his head, interrupting her.

She sighed. "I'm sorry. I'm babbling. I just wanted to see you so much, and now that you're here—well, I feel like I've got to say everything at once."

"You got time."

"No, you'll disappear again."

Anna watched the way he grinned, and she knew it was true. She said, "Then just let me say that everybody is grateful and that I am so happy to see you again." She smiled up at him. "I hope you feel proud."

"You know what it's like?"

She shook her head.

"Well, all my life I been running away. If something's hard or if it don't feel right, I just had one answer— run away. Anyway, this is one time in my life when I didn't." He squinted as if he had said more than he wanted to. He turned his baseball cap in his hands. "Anyway, it's something to look back on."

"For us too."

There was a pause, and then Uncle Newt said, "Well, I just wanted to drop by for a minute. I figured you'd be back here by yourself, getting ready to sell records. I didn't want to leave without saying good-bye."

"You're going?"

He nodded.

"Where, Uncle Newt? Will we see you again?"

"You remember George Oatis?"

"No."

"Him and me grew up together. It's his car I was driving the night of the accident. Anyway, it's too many people around here for us, and Oats says he knows a man who can get us jobs out West."

"You mean, like cowboys?"

Uncle Newt put his baseball cap on his head, grinned and ducked in embarrassment. "We probably sound like two fools to you."

"No."

"We sound like fools to ourselves. I don't guess we'll bust broncos or anything."

"I just hope you'll be happy, and I'm really glad I got to know you."

"That goes double for me."

Anna started to reach out to him, to shake his hand, but something about the way he was standing stopped her. "Listen," she said suddenly, "do you need money? I've got a hundred and twenty-eight dollars over there in the box. I'd be glad to give it to you. The whole family would.''

"No.''

"They'd be honored if you took it, really.''

"No!'' He lifted his hands. "No, thank you.'' He lowered his hands, palms down, as if he were pressing something back into a box. "I want to leave things between me and your family just exactly where they're at. If that makes any sense.'' He took a step toward the door. "Now, you take care of yourself, you hear?''

"I will. You too.''

At the door he shifted his weight and paused. Without looking at her, he said, "You're the best of the bunch—you know that?''

The way he said it, as if it were the first compliment he had ever given anybody, took her breath. She said in a rush, "I'm not, but thank you for saying it.''

He turned his head and looked directly at her. "It's true. Any one of them—your mom, Bubba, any one of them would give me money now. Would be glad to. But you would have done it before, wouldn't you?''

"Yes.''

"See, I knew that. I could tell. You've got a generous, kind way about you, and don't you ever lose it.'' She couldn't answer. "Well, you tell the family I said so long.''

"I will, Uncle Newt.''

He touched the brim of his baseball cap and went out

119

the door. It swung shut slowly behind him.

Anna stood for a moment in the empty entrance hall. She waited, listening for the sound of Uncle Newt's car driving away. When the sound faded, she turned to go back into the auditorium.

As she turned she glanced up at George Washington. He seemed to be watching her with his bright blue eyes. She stepped closer.

Whoever had made the plaster statue had left the eyes blank, but someone had ballpoint-penned in some blue pupils. Suddenly she liked the statue. She looked up at it again. She put one hand on the cold plaster. There were probably a hundred statues like this in George Washington High Schools all over the country. And yet this one had, just by waiting, gotten a personality.

Smiling slightly, she turned to the auditorium. As she took the last seat, she heard her father saying, "We're going to take a short break now—doctor's orders—and while we do, at the back of the auditorium, one of the Glory girls, our little Anna, will be waiting to help you with your purchases. Stand up, darling, so they can see where you're at."

Anna got up. For the first time in her life she stood up smiling. She waved her hand and then stepped back out the auditorium door and sat at her table.

She straightened the stacks of records and cassette tapes. Her uncle's words, "You're the best of the bunch," still echoed in her mind, making her feel better each time she heard them. "You've got a generous, kind way about you." It was as if he had given her the first two positive pieces of a large and complicated puzzle. Like George Washington, she was at last getting a personality. Her smile broadened as the first people came out of the auditorium. "Can I help you?" she asked.

"Tonight before we sing our closing theme song, I'd like to say a special word about my brother, Newt. It was him that saved our lives. He put his life on the line again and again, for each one of us, and I wanted Newt to be with us tonight, singing here on the stage, part of the Glory family at last. It couldn't be. So tonight I want to go on record as saying this. Wherever you are, Newt, whatever you're doing, anytime you want to, come on home and—

> "Sing with the Glorys
> Yes, come sing
> With the Glorys
> If you sing
> With the Glorys
> Then you'll never,
> Never,
> Never!
> Sing a-lone!

"Good night, everybody, and may God bless you and keep you until we meet again."

121

ABOUT THE AUTHOR

Betsy Byars was born in Charlotte, North Carolina, and lived there until her graduation from Queens College.

The mother of four, Mrs. Byars began writing books for children as her own family was growing up. She is the author of many books, including *The Summer of the Swans*, which received the Newbery Award.

Mrs. Byars now lives in South Carolina, where her husband is associated with Clemson University. She and her husband have traveled widely throughout the United States in pursuit of their interest in gliding and antique airplanes.